WORLD'S END: THE TWIN FILES

Lucas Kawamoto

THE ALPS, SWITZERLAND
JUNE 27, 2037

ONE

Don't hesitate.

That's the rule. Since day one. From the beginning of training. In the field, everything relies on your timing, on your ability to react. You have to adapt before the situation gets you killed.

A heavy gale breezes across the mountaintop as I adjust the scope of my sniper rifle thirty degrees to the right. I narrow my right eye and shift my crouched stance ever so slightly. My gaze travels thirteen hundred meters down towards a set of rails winding along the mountain range, searching for signs of the convoy I'm waiting for.

After three and a half minutes, the steel cars of the cargo train come into sight. I take aim at the connection point between the lead car and the rest. I reach to my waist and grab a circular disk. I hold it in my hand and tap twice with my thumb. This device sends geothermal waves through metal as it connects. I'm going to use it to sever the car from the rest.

My stomach clenches as I steady myself. The train is downwind—to make the shot, I'll have to time it perfectly for the disk to hit the connection point.

The train comes around the mountain parallel to the one I'm on, weaving its way up the tracks toward the peak, where a research center lies. The convoy is carrying a highly valuable asset our director must have to move forward with the project. So, my assignment—get the asset out of the cargo train as quickly as possible. That starts with me immobilizing the cars.

My brow furrows in concentration as the train comes around for a wide-open pass. This will be my best chance of making the shot. I start a silent countdown for five seconds in my head. I hold the sniper completely still, aiming ahead of the connection.

Three, two, one. I pull the trigger, and the shot flies across the open canyon. It sends a recoil through the rifle, jolting my body. I quickly recover and line my eye up with the scope. The shot flies for several long seconds before it hits. The metal of the connection point slowly starts to melt. The first train car pulls away from the rest of the convoy, and the final cars slow to a stop on the rails. I hear shouts from inside the train. I see a group of men climb up to the roof of one of the cars holding machine guns in their hands. I turn my sniper rifle towards them and send a shot flying at one of them. The bullet hits him directly below his chin, and he clutches his neck, blood splattering out and onto the roof of the car. I reload and fire at a second man without hesitation, the shot piercing cleanly through his forehead.

I pull my sniper forward and shoot another before he can enter the car. He falls backward, and his body tumbles down the cliff. I've done my part. A strike team will take care of the asset on board the train. I have to escape—now. The extraction point is seven kilometers east, in a small town called Ewen. I turn my attention back to the main car.

The strike team is now moving in, and as I angle my sniper rifle upwards at the cliff above the rails, I spot the outlines of fifteen men rappelling toward the train. I stay and watch as they land on the roof of the cargo train cars. They drop down inside the train and disappear from view.

I know I'm supposed to head for the extraction point, but something holds me here. I wait for several quiet minutes until I start to feel anxious. The strike team should be out by now. Something's wrong.

I watch as the panels of one of the trains slide open. Men dressed in black climb out, each holding a member of the strike team at gunpoint. I swallow, shifting my stance. Finally, an authoritative man gives an order, and even from across the canyon, I can hear the sound of their gunshots.

They knew we were coming.

I quickly disassemble my sniper rifle, storing the components in a small sheath, which I strap to my leg. Those men certainly know my location by now.

I start running down the steep rocky path that leads down from the mountaintop. If I can make it to the bottom before the men arrive, I'll be able to get away on my motorcycle towards the extraction point. Protocol dictates that in case of mission failure, the extraction window narrows by fifteen minutes. I'll have to be fast.

After five minutes, I reach the base of the mountain, sweat beading on my forehead. I climb onto my motorcycle and turn on the engine. I drive down the road that leads to the rest of the city, my eyes watching for any sign of the soldiers.

I continue down the road, wedged in between two neighboring mountains. I push the vehicle to go faster, and soon I reach a tunnel nestled into the side of a steep cliff. I pass through it, my eyes adjusting to the dark. The only sources of light are the glowing yellow orbs that lie along the edge of the tunnel. I look forward, seeing that the tunnel easily stretches for another two miles.

The sound of other engines comes from behind me. I swallow, taking a glance backward. Three other motorcycles are following close behind, each with a man dressed in black armor riding on them. I hear the sound of gunshots ring out as they raise their pistols to open fire.

I swerve to the side of the tunnel, bullets ricocheting off the sloping walls behind me. I steer my motorcycle from side to side in an attempt to make myself a harder target to hit. More gunshots sound from behind, and I cringe as one of the lights directly above my head shatters into shards of glass. Soon I come up to the end of the tunnel. The darkness transforms into broad daylight, making me more visible to my pursuers. I hear one of them nearing closer and closer, and when I chance a look behind, I grimace as one of the motorcycles has drawn within ten meters. Unholstering my gun, I pivot on my seat, keeping my left hand on the handlebar. I narrow my eyes, then fire several shots back at him. One of the bullets hits the soldier square in the chest, and he tumbles backward off his motorcycle.

Up ahead, a long bridge crosses over a wide gorge that spans the distance between this road and the town. Down below, a waterfall cascades into a long, winding river that leads to the ocean. Across the steel bridge lies Ewen. My eyes focus on a large tower on the outskirts of the city. That's my extraction point.

I notice a large gray lever lying at the end of the bridge. I frown. Then it dawns upon me that the city of Ewen used to be much lower in the ground until the government had it raised up several hundred feet. Boats used to pass through this river to the town, so the bridge must have been able to open to let them through.

An idea forms in my mind.

The motorcycle's engine roars as I turn the throttle harder. I race across the bridge, nearing the lever. Bullets fly through the air, narrowly missing me. I reach the lever and slide off the motorcycle. I run to the lever and pull on it as hard as I can.

A groaning noise sounds from the bridge, and the clank of metal gears reaches my ears. The two halves of the bridge slowly begin to rise upwards, and the men chasing me are forced to a stop.

Not looking back, I climb onto my motorcycle once more and head for the extraction point. Once I reach the city, I enter through a small side road, avoiding the crowds of tourists pushing through the main gates. The alley that I take is narrow and bumpy, the concrete of the road itself being made up of dense pebbles.

As I exit the alley, I'm forced onto a main road filled with people heading to the marketplace. I turn my motorcycle to make a hard right, continuing to head in the direction of the tower. I weave through the tourists on the street, trying to blend in with them in order to avoid being followed.

Within minutes I reach the large tower that acts as the extraction point. The building itself is made up of graying brick, constructed over sixty years ago. The main archway that leads into the tower is lined with angels made of stone, and I have to leave my motorcycle behind to make it inside.

The interior of the tower has a large room at the base, with several older men and women sitting inside, reading newspapers. I hurry up a flight of spiral stairs, heading up the levels toward the top. I run up at least seven staircases before reaching the top floor, where I pause and take several long breaths in exhaustion.

I can hear the sound of a bell ringing above my head, and I realize that this old building must act as the town's clock tower. In the corner of the room, I spot a rickety wooden ladder that leads up above. I climb up the ladder and push open a circular hatch.

As I emerge from the inside of the building, beams of sunlight hit my face. I come out onto a large platform overlooking the rest of the city. To my left lies a massive metal bell that hangs from the connection point between the four archways above me.

The sound of rotors spinning reaches me as I realize that the chopper must be here now. I take several steps to the left to gaze out at the city, where I spot a sleek black helicopter moving toward me. When the pilot spots me, he swerves to the right towards the clock tower and pulls up close. The side panel of the chopper slides open, and a woman throws a long rope with a carabiner at the end. I catch the rope with ease and hook the clipped end to my belt. Once I'm secured, I take a quick step off the side of the rooftop, where I dangle in midair. I hear the crank of a winch, and the rope begins to reel me upwards. When I reach the chopper's belly, I grab hold of the landing skids and pull myself up. The woman extends a hand to me, and I step into the helicopter's cargo hold.

I settle into a seat near the corner of the chopper, taking the sheath that holds my sniper rifle and placing it on a rack. The woman who helped me earlier sits down and makes eye contact.

"As I'm sure you have gathered by now, the mission you were sent on was a setup, and Laurings' men knew we were going to intercept their train. There was a breach at one of our lockdown facilities." She draws in a deep breath. "Laurings has escaped."

TWO

stare at my phone for several moments, my heart rate rising as my finger hovers over the call button. The contact reads SKYE WALKER.

I haven't called her in over two years. She left the NAIS after London happened. The mission seemed simple. Trying to save the kidnapped daughter of some wealthy philanthropist. I was shot en route to the meeting point. By the time Skye got there, it was too late. The captors panicked and shot the girl. Skye blamed herself. She still does. She left the agency in pursuit of a regular life where the only person she'd have to look out for was herself.

But now, I need her. There's no one I trust more. Oscar Laurings, a dangerous and accomplished mercenary renowned in crime circles across the globe, has escaped from prison and is after two of the most important pieces of information in the world. The Vice Director and my commander, Evelyn Taylor, has assigned me the task of tracking him down. I need a partner for this mission.

I tap the call button. I wait about twenty seconds as it rings, my jaw clenched, wondering if she'll pick up. Then I hear her voice.

"August?"

I swallow. I haven't heard her voice in so long.

When I don't answer, she continues. "I know there's something you need from me," she adds. "Tell me, and we'll see if we can work something out."

I clear my throat. "It's about Oscar Laurings."

I can picture her contemplating that; her lips curved into a frown. I hear a door shutting.

"Alright," she replies. "What is it?"

"Oscar Laurings escaped the Red Diamond lockdown prison yesterday at 1200 hours. We believe he's after the Twin Files."

Another pause. My right leg begins to shake. For a second, I think she's going to hang up, but then I hear her voice once more.

"I take it that you want my help finding him?"

"Yes." Her thought process is still quick. "Skye, you're the best agent I've ever known. There are so many lives at stake here, and there's no one that I trust more than you."

More silence. I can tell that the compliment jarred her.

"Okay," she says. "Where should I find you?"

I heave a sigh of relief, not caring that she'll hear it. "LAX Airfield 19B. Tell the guards I sent you, and give them the chain code 1D4PX."

"Got it."

Skye's waiting for me as I pull in through the gate. As soon as the car stops, I step out and onto the tarmac. She greets me with a hug, which surprises me.

I step back, taking a good look at her. She looks mostly the same as I remember her: Light brown hair pulled back into a bun, deep blue eyes, an expression on her face that fills the gap in-between friendly and dangerous.

"Hi, Skye."

"Hi, August," she replies. "How are you?"

"Mostly well. You?"

She shrugs and looks around the airfield, even though I'm confident she's already surveyed it in its entirety. "Are we going somewhere?"

"Follow me."

A huge military plane lies in the center of the airstrip. Its wide cargo bay door is folded down. Men rush back and forth from the massive vehicle, carrying various pumps and other pieces of equipment. Large guns protrude from the bottom of each wing, where small cranes are installing boxes of ammunition into their back compartments.

Soldiers salute as we walk up the ramp onto the plane. I climb a flight of stairs to the main deck, Skye trailing behind me.

We both settle down into armchairs at the head of the plane.

"We're good to go," I say to an officer, and she disappears behind the cockpit door.

I look at Skye. "As I told you earlier, the White House vault was raided by a group of Laurings' men. The Director has given me a lead on Laurings, and I want your help to find him."

She doesn't reply immediately. The director, Luke Walker, is her father. He was furious when she left the agency. That just made her want out even more.

"What does this mission involve?"

I swallow. "It's high-stakes, meaning the limited resources we have are all going into this mission. The operation itself involves a sky-drop in the Alps near one of Laurings' military bases. We believe that Laurings himself was recently there and that if we go and get the intel we need, we'll be able to find his current location."

"Just us?"

"That's the idea. The Director wants us to be in and out."

Skye slowly nods. "Seems simple enough."

I'm still surprised that she's agreed to come along on the mission, especially considering what happened between us after that last mission. I can still remember how she had cried for hours on end, screaming at the world while leaning on my shoulder. The day after the mission, she apologized and told me she was leaving the agency.

I nod in return, then stare out the window as the cargo ramp lifts up and closes. "We'll be in Europe in no less than seven hours. We should try to get some sleep." I glance back at her. "This mission will be dangerous, so we're going to need all the rest we can get."

THREE

"Listen up."

Jayson, our mission briefer, holds up a parachute in each hand. Each one is marked with a different symbol, and the layers of metal and cloth are noticeably separate. Skye nods.

"Each of these is meant for a different job. This first one," he raises the one in his right hand, "is your altitude glider. When you jump out of the cargo hold and reach deployment altitude, you'll open it. That should get you to the level you need to use your second parachute." Jayson nods at the one in his left hand. "This parachute will get you across the open plateau and onto the ridge without being seen. It's equipped with micro-fibers that use the wind to their advantage. If you reach the correct point with your first parachute, this one will get you across the plateau in under a minute."

"So if everything goes according to plan, the first parachute will get us to a drop zone, and from there, we deploy the second parachute, which will get us across the plateau?" I ask, hoping the plan is as simple as it sounds.

"Correct," he replies. "The cargo hold's doors will open in twenty-five minutes, and in that time, we'll equip you with everything you need for the mission. All the equipment we have can be dropped during your jump, so you don't have to carry excess weight. Follow me."

He leads us down the stairs and into the cargo hold, where a rack of parachutes hangs, as well as a table littered with guns and explosives. The cargo hold stretches back around twenty meters to the massive cargo bay doors.

Jayson moves to the table. He picks up a pistol, fingering it in his hand.

He turns toward us, giving us a clear view of the weapon. "These are lightweight and versatile; they can be coded to your unique biometrics. Trackers have been installed but can terminate if you squeeze the bullet chamber three times in succession. You'll each be carrying one of these."

He walks over to Skye and hands her one. Then he hands me mine. I watch as the fingerprint sensors on the handle of the pistol flash green as I tighten my grip. It feels light in my hand, and I turn it over to find the bullet chamber. I find a clip already installed, and I pull it out, studying the size. Twenty-shots. Pretty generous mag size for a weapon this small—Jayson was right. This will be useful during the mission.

"Next up." Jayson hands us a belt full of rectangular-shaped explosives.

I pull mine over my head and loop it across one shoulder so that it crosses my chest. Skye does the same.

"These are high-impact explosives." Jayson hands us each a small cylindrical console. "They're strong enough to break through inches of thick steel and can all be accessed by those consoles I gave you. Strap the consoles to your wrist for easy access."

I strap the console to my wrist. When I tap the screen, it lights up with symbols and numbers representing individual explosives.

"Listen carefully," Jayson says. "The panel that I gave you will also display your current altitude."

I glance at the console. As he said, it shows a shifting number on the screen.

Jayson continues, "At 2300 meters, I want you to pull the tab for the first parachute. From there, the screen will display your trajectory towards the point you need to reach."

He also hands us a set of earbuds and a small microphone. I put the earbuds in my ears and tuck the microphone to the side of my head, nestling it into my hair.

"That's it?" Skye asks, tightening the straps on her wrist.

"All but the parachutes." Jayson holds up a set of parachutes and hands them to me. "Both of you should know how to use these. They're outfitted with the exact same custom controls that you used in training; I'll guide you through the flight via the earbuds."

"That sounds good to me," I say. "How long until launch time?"

"Fifteen minutes." Jayson looks at us. "Take the time to rest and prepare for the mission. This won't be easy."

Skye and I exchange a glance. Nothing could be more true. The plan is simple but requires everything to go exactly as planned. One mistake could mean death. And every decision we make could help determine the fate of the agency.

The time passes quickly. I try to relax and not worry, but I always come back to the possibility of failure.

But then, it's time.

Jayson and several others are waiting for us. They outfit us with light black jumpsuits, which allow our guns and explosives to be tightly strapped to us. A young man helps me with my parachute, telling me which tabs to pull when and showing me how to discard my first parachute for the second.

After two minutes, we're fully outfitted. Skye and I stand next to each other at the far end of the cargo bay, and the beeping sound of the cargo door opening jars me. I stare out at the immense blue sky, the clouds covering the mountains below from sight. The wind knocks me off balance, and I pull a pair of goggles over my head, shielding my eyes from the heavy gale.

"Ready?" I ask Skye.

"Ready."

I take several cautious steps toward the edge of the cargo bay. I look down at the clouds, keeping my balance. I've never been afraid of heights, and now, the daunting drop to the ground below still doesn't bother me. Skye walks up next to me, and I nod at her.

And then I step over the edge.

Skydiving is an experience that you can't explain to those who haven't done it before. The intense wind hits me hard, knocking the breath out of my chest. I fall towards the ground, my arms flailing wildly.

I take control.

I tuck my arms at my side, forming an arrowhead with my body. I cut through the air at a much sharper angle and, as a result, a much faster speed. I feel my hair flying around, and as I plummet down past the clouds, I get my first glimpse of the Andes. The mountains are covered in snow, small patches of brown and green contrasting heavily with the barren white slopes. The beautiful scenery continues farther than I can see. The air is much thinner at this altitude, and I find myself heaving for breath.

I turn my head to the right and spot Skye diving down about ten meters away from me. I angle myself slightly to the left, aiming for a valley covered in pine trees. I glance at my console, which displays the number five thousand on it. At

2300 meters, I need to pull my parachute's deployment tab.

Barely a minute passes before the number turns to 3000. I ready myself, placing my hand on the tab. The number rapidly gets smaller, and I tense when the number hits 2500.

The numbers keep changing. 2450. 2420. 2400.

I swallow hard. 2350. 2325. 2300.

I yank the tab as hard as I can. I feel myself slow down, and the chute unfurls behind me, catching wind. My flight becomes more streamlined, and when I glance behind, I'm relieved to see the white fabric of the parachute folded outwards. I look at my wrist, and the console is flashing green, indicating a successful deployment. It flickers once, then displays a map of my flight path.

I steer myself towards the mountains, letting the parachute do most of the work. Next to me, Skye has also deployed her glider successfully.

After around three minutes of smooth flight, we reach the point where our second glider needs to be deployed. I find the tab near my waist and pull. It doesn't move an inch. I yank on it hard again, frowning to see that it still won't budge. My eyes move toward my waist. The chute's caught on my belt. Shit.

I try to wrench it free to no avail. I grit my teeth. Even if I were to get it free, the chute would be useless because I would have to tear through the fabric in order to separate the tab from my belt. I still have my first parachute working. I quickly formulate a plan.

The second glider is useless to me now. I watch ahead as a large canyon comes into sight. To one side, lying across an open plateau, I see a looming gray structure nestled into the side of a cliff. The base. My eyes narrow as I spot a ridge towards the end of the open plain. That's where we're supposed to land. But I won't be able to make it there now, as my second parachute has failed. I also can't land on the plateau. They'll see me too easily.

The only other option is the cliff.

If I can time it right, I can steer my glider low enough so the guards around the base won't see me. I'll have to land on the cliffside and find a hold within the span of a few seconds. I would then have to climb sideways across the cliff face in order to reach the ridge without being seen. It's a risky plan, but I don't have any other options.

"August, your trajectory is off by over a hundred meters," Jayson says in my ear. "Why haven't you deployed your second glider?"

"My chute is jammed," I reply. "I'm going to try and land on the cliff. Then I'll make my way over to the ridge. Skye, can you wait for me there?"

"That's risky, August. Do you have any other options?"

"Negative."

Skye takes a deep breath. "Alright then, good luck. I'll start recon at the ridge while I wait."

The comms go silent once more, replaced by the howl of the wind.

I keep myself focused, with my first glider still allowing me to steer. I position myself so that I'm heading directly toward a small outcrop of rocks around two-thirds of the way up the cliff. If I'm lucky, I'll be able to land there. When I hit the cliff, I'll need to cut my parachute off because it'll pull me backward. I fumble for my knife, which is tucked into a small pocket in my pants. I manage to secure a hold of it despite the wind.

I reach the cliff and grab hold of a sturdy-looking branch. My arm scrapes hard against stone as I do so. I manage to find a small ledge for my feet, and I try to steady myself. I quickly cut the left string of my parachute, but as I move to slice the right side free, the uneven weight distribution throws me off balance. My feet slip from the ledge, and I find myself falling.

I'm barely able to grab onto a loose vine before I completely lose control. The stop causes my whole body to snap tightly, and I clench my jaw from the pain. I scramble for footholds on the cliffside, and my parachute threatens to pull me off once more. I take my knife and cut through the parachute again, securing my hold on the side of the cliff.

I heave several long breaths, keeping my body pressed against the steep cliff face. Then I remember the mission and force myself to begin climbing.

The process is slow and grueling. I slowly make my way up the cliff, moving each of my limbs in a practiced motion. After almost thirty minutes of climbing, I glimpse the top of the cliff. Now for the next step in my plan, which will require coordination and patience. Once I'm at the top, I need to reach the ridge west of me. In order to do that, I'll have to climb sideways across the cliff.

Climbing sideways isn't like climbing up or down. I have to keep myself steady through every move, making sure that I have a secure hold before I move one of my hands to the left. I make it to the ridge in just over ten minutes.

As I pull myself over the edge of the cliff, I find Skye waiting for me, a pair of binoculars in hand. It appears as though she's been surveilling the base. She breathes a sigh of relief when she sees me.

"You made it," she says, helping me up.

I raise my eyebrows. "Did you ever really doubt me?"

Skye shrugs. "Not really," she replies, turning towards the ridge and motioning for me to follow her.

She leads us up a short trail to the top of the ridge. The base is across from us, maybe eight hundred meters from our position. I can see the outlines of the guards as they move back and forth across the base's walkways.

"They move in a rotation of every fifteen minutes," Skye points at the guards. "Each of them is equipped with DC-12 Assault Rifles, and they all wear earbuds connected to the same channel. Our best shot at moving in is near the end of their rotation. They'll be the most off-guard at that point, and it'll provide the best opening for us that there is."

"Sounds good. Do you have a plan to get into the base, or does the original work well enough?"

She turns toward me. "Well, here's the thing. Originally we thought that their rotation period was every thirty minutes, which would have made it easier to go through the west entrance. But now we know that they rotate positions in a much shorter amount of time. I believe that the easiest way for us to get in now would be by rappelling."

I smile. She's retained so many mission assessment skills after so long. "Alright," I say. "We have the gear, so we can do it. Which entrance would we go in through, though?"

Skye grins. "Who said anything about going in through an entrance? We should land on the top of the building. The security is minimalistic on the roof, which will work perfectly to our advantage."

"So, in order to rappel into the base, we have to make our way up the mountainside, correct?"

"Correct—we should get moving."

After so many months of being away from the agency, Skye has clearly picked up her old skills again. It's like she never left. I resent what happened that caused her to leave the agency. To leave me.

The path we take up the mountain is long and steep. We had to take a wide loop back from the ridge in order to avoid being seen by the base's guards. Now we've almost reached the top of the tall peak, and I keep my eyes forward, not daring to look over the edge of the steep cliff.

Once we reach the top, we unload our equipment from our belts. I loop my rope through my belt and clip it in two places to ensure safety. These ropes were made for this and are comprised of heavy Kevlar, which is strong bulletproof material able to withstand almost anything. We tie our ropes tightly onto several massive trees, using screws to hold them in place.

After everything has been set up, we move to the edge of the cliff. I kneel on the side, keeping a grip on my rope. I place my hands on the edge, keeping a firm hold, then swing my right leg over the edge and onto the cliff face. This cliff is steep, almost at an eighty-degree angle. I keep the rope in my hand and then move my left leg over the edge. The only thing that is keeping me in place is my hands, which are now above me as I hang over the side. I then straighten myself so that the rope is directly in front of me. I'm ready to rappel down.

Next to me, Skye has done the same thing. We nod to each other.

I push my feet off hard against the cliff face. I feel myself launched backward into the air. A second passes where I'm suspended and falling before I swing back into the cliff, the force of the impact jarring my bones. I push off once more, again being catapulted backward in midair.

This process of swinging back and forth downwards continues for almost three whole minutes. When I realize that we're nearing the bottom of the cliff, I stop myself from going any further. The rope tied around my waist holds taut, and I move myself closer to the cliff. Turning my head, I look downwards at the roof of the base. The cliff continues downwards for around fifteen meters and then stops abruptly, turning into the gray concrete of the base's roof. Three guards armed with guns are patrolling back and forth across it, spread apart by around twenty meters. The only cover visible to me is a set of satellite dishes and a small structure surrounding the elevator that leads downwards into the base.

I watch the guards quietly, contemplating our next move. Skye reaches my same position on the cliff, and she, too, studies the rooftop down below. She looks up at me, and I give her a signal, indicating that I'm ready to move in. She nods back silently.

My movement is calculated and quick. I rappel down twice more, then stop nearly above the rooftop. I then unclip myself from the rope, and I land quietly on the hard concrete, rolling to soften the impact. Skye lands next to me, and we each move forward in a fast, crouched position. The guards are still continuing their patrol, and I move in behind one of the satellites. I reach for my holster and slide out my gun. Skye holds up two fingers and moves them from side to side. She's going to cause a distraction while I move in and take down the guards.

Skye hits the satellite dish next to her twice with the handle of her gun. I hear the guard's voices in confusion, followed by their footsteps. I silence my pistol with the twist of a knob and wait. The guards, all three of them, move toward Skye, where they had heard the sound. As they do, I emerge from behind my satellite dish. I come out behind them, and they don't see me. I raise my gun and fire on two of them. The bullets hit them both hard in the chest, and they stumble down. The third turns toward me, and as he does, Skye comes out from behind him and throws a knife into his chest with deadly precision. The guard collapses onto the ground. I reach down to his body and pull a keycard from his jacket pocket.

I don't think about the lives that I took, remembering that this mission needs to be executed without hesitation. Without a word, Skye and I move away from the bodies of the fallen guards and towards the elevator. Skye takes out the security camera without being seen, creating a shower of sparks as she fires at it with her pistol. I swipe the keycard along a scanner next to the elevator, and the metal doors slide open smoothly. Before we step in, I check the elevator's ceilings for any hidden cameras. When I spot one in the corner, I quickly send a bullet into it. Skye steps inside, and I follow her in.

"Nice work," I tell her as the elevator doors close behind us.

Skye nods back. "You too." She pauses for a second, reloading her gun with a fresh clip. "The logging area is likely near us, on the east side." The logging section of the base is the area where Laurings' location record will be kept. "The security there won't be too heavy, but we'll still have to be careful."

"Agreed. But the logging section was designed specifically for minimal cover, to allow the guards to have the most advantage possible. But our best shot at breaking in will be by taking down the guards without any gunfire. The element of surprise will be key in allowing us to create the largest amount of confusion," I say.

"Alright then," she says. "Let's move in."

The doors to the elevator slide open without a sound. I step out into a long hallway with plain walls and start moving left. Skye follows me, and the two of us make our way through the base slowly. We come around a bend, where a guard is standing. I hold up a hand at Skye, and she nods.

The guard is facing away from me right now, and I creep forward, keeping my steps short and silent. When I reach him, I place my hands quickly onto his head and twist. His neck snaps, and he falls. Moving quickly, I catch his body before it hits the ground. Skye and I drag him away and into a storage closet.

After shutting the closet door, Skye and I continue making our way down the hall, our guard up. I round the corner, my eyes narrowed ahead. Another plain white hallway lies in front of us, and at the end of it is a steel walkway that leads across a narrow gorge.

We cross the short bridge as quickly as we can. We're exposed. The heavy wind threatens to push me off balance, and when we reach the other end, the gale goes away, replaced by the heat of the next interior hallway. I frown, seeing that the hallway is empty, with not a single guard in sight. Skye seems to notice this as well. Something about this is much too quiet.

I pull my gun from my holster, keeping it angled downward in a defensive position. Next to me, Skye does the same. We move in unison down the hallway, keeping our steps as light as possible. At the end of the hallway lies a large metal door. Next to it on the wall is a plaque that reads RECORDS AND LOGGING. I nod at Skye. This is the place.

I swipe the keycard I found earlier along the scanner that lies under the plaque. It flashes red, and I swallow. A small beeping noise sounds from a device on the wall, and Skye and I tense, knowing full well that we have alerted the security system to our presence.

The drum of several footsteps sounds from another hallway that connects to the one we're in. They're coming from a second door that lies next to the one with the scanner. This door has no scanner on it, meaning that it leads to somewhere without any security clearance requirements.

I hold up two fingers to Skye and gesture to either side of the door. She nods, and we each move to one side of the door where the footsteps came from. When the soldiers come in, we'll be able to take them by surprise.

Several seconds pass, the footsteps coming nearer. Without any warning, the door bursts open, and two soldiers walk into our hallway, looking for any signs of us. It's clear that they didn't see us when they came in, and we emerge behind them from our places next to the door.

I swing my leg up onto one of their shoulders and pull myself up with ease, twisting my leg into a tight hold around his neck. I push him to the ground, my leg still wrapped around his neck. I push in on my leg, squeezing his neck. He gasps, his face turning a shade of purple. After several seconds he falls unconscious, and I stand up.

Next to me, Skye has also taken out her soldier, who lies unconscious as well. She searches their body for any sort of card that might allow us into the room with the locked door. I do the same with my soldier, but I find nothing.

"Did you bring the explosives?" I ask her, standing back up from the soldier's body.

"A couple of these should bring down that door," Skye says, pulling several blocks of C4 from a sling that wraps around her shoulder. "Though we'll only have around a minute before they send more security to check this area."

She hands me one of the explosives, and we each place one on each side of the door, making sure that the hinges will be blown when they detonate.

We both back up to the end of the hallway, and Skye taps her arm console.

The explosion shakes the ground, and the metal door slams to the ground. The walls of the hallway burst alight with flames, and I rush towards the fallen door, my gun up.

Skye and I step inside the vast room. It's a large space, with a set of computers lined up on a table to the right. A guard at the corner of the room springs up from his seat, firing his gun at us. I roll sideways away from Skye, raising my own gun. I don't hesitate, shooting the soldier twice in the chest.

My eyes travel to the center of the room, where a massive screen lies in midair, projected from a device on the wall. The emblem of the Shadow Group is displayed prominently, and a set of words are written under it. This is where the records are kept and where we can find Laurings' location.

I walk forward toward it, unsure how the hologram functions. I raise my hands, tapping on an option on the screen that reads RECORD OF ALL ARRIVALS AND DEPARTURES. My hands seemingly phase through the hologram, but the hologram reacts as though I had interacted with it physically.

The screen changes to display a long list of names followed by a set of times and locations. My eyes skim over the list, recognizing some of the names as I search for the letter L. Finally, I find the name Laurings, Oscar among the names, and I look at the times he departed.

It seems as though Laurings arrived at this particular base just a day ago and departed late this morning. That means we just missed him. But that doesn't concern me—what does is that Laurings current location is blacked out on the screen, clearly meant to hide where he is.

Skye notices this too, and she turns toward me. I frown, thinking of other options.

"Can you get through the firewall?" I ask her.

Skye nods. "I can do it. But it'll take time."

"Alright," I reply. "I'll hold off the guards as long as I can. Try to be quick."

As Skye moves to the computers in the corner of the room, I turn toward the broken-down door, pulling a set of batons from my belt. I hear shouts coming from outside, and I know the best chance I have of giving Skye more time is to move into the hallway to fight them. So I step into the hallway.

The first things I see are several guards rushing down the hallway toward me. I twist the batons together, locking them into place. They're a special set of weapons designed especially for fights like these. The two batons are linked together in the center by a handlebar, and they can be pulled off. When they are, a rope made of heavy Kevlar extends with them, and one of the special functions of the batons is linked to the rope.

The guards lift their guns, taking aim at me. Before they can open fire, I pull one of the batons from the main handlebar, where the other baton is still attached. I swing the detached baton forward toward the guard closest to me. The rope extends with it, and the lightweight bar flies forward toward the soldier, striking him in the chest. I squeeze the center handlebar, and the rope reels in, connecting the two batons together once more.

I slide to my knees, narrowly avoiding a full clip of bullets. Once more, I detach one of the batons and whirl it toward the next soldier. The rope trails out farther this time, and I twist so that the rope wraps around his neck. Sliding up onto my feet again, I pull hard on the main handle. The soldier collapses, clutching their throat.

I run towards the fallen soldier, reeling the rope back in. The baton flies back into my hand, and I connect it to the main section once again. I swing my leg forward into his head, knocking him unconscious. I lift the fallen soldier using one of my arms, using his back, which is covered in a bulletproof vest, as a shield. Two more soldiers round the corner, opening fire. I crouch, propping the soldier's body up on my knee. The bullets deflect easily off his vest, and I continue to shield myself from the oncoming fire.

After I hear the last bullet of a clip ring out, I race forward with the body, still protecting my body from the soldiers. As they reload their guns, I drop the soldier's body and detach one of the batons. I swing it forward horizontally, the baton making a sideways arc before it catches one of the soldiers in the stomach. He groans, clutching his chest, and I immediately follow up the hit by pulling the second baton from the main handle and throwing it. Now the only thing I hold is the center handle that connects the two by the rope, and I squeeze it twice. This activates the special function of the batons, and I hear a whirring noise as the two ropes begin to spin.

The two batons begin to spin in a circle around me, and I hold the center handlebar vertically so that the rope is swinging the batons in front of me. This effectively creates a moving circle in front of me, and as the final soldier opens fire on me, the metal rope cuts through the bullets, easily deflecting them before they can hit me.

The final soldier stops firing for a second to load in a new clip, and I take this opportunity to cease the spinning function. Within half a second, the rope stops moving the batons in a circle, and the two bars return to the center handle. I quickly detach the one closer to me and swing it forward straight into the soldier. He collapses onto the ground from the impact.

The baton returns to me, and I attach it back to the main handlebar. Clipping the batons back onto my belt, I heave a breath of exhaustion, wiping beads of sweat from my forehead. I turn towards the logging room and rush back through the broken door, hoping Skye has found something.

Skye looks up from a computer at my entrance, then stands and runs toward me. She has a slight smile on her lips, and I hope that means she's broken into the system.

"I found Laurings," she says eagerly, meeting me in the center of the room. "After searching through the files for several minutes, I was able to trace his location all the way to the city of Tokyo in Japan."

I swallow, not sure what to think of this. Tokyo is a large city with many small places where Laurings could be hiding. It'll be hard to find him there, especially with how many contacts he has.

Skye notices my expression and tells me something that gets my hopes up. "Don't worry, I found what he's doing there. Laurings is attending a business meeting with the Chief Executive Officer of a military company known as Leonard Industries. He seems to be partnering with them for some sort of arms exchange, and from what I could tell, he's buying hundreds of missiles."

I frown. Something about the name of that company feels familiar to me. After thinking for several seconds, I remember why I know Leonard Industries. Several years ago, the director sent me on a mission to recover three nuclear missiles from Beijing. The company that had made those missiles was Leonard Industries, a large name in the military industry.

But what that company does matters to me more than the familiarity of its name. Leonard Industries manufactures the most advanced nuclear warheads in the world, and if Laurings is trying to buy from them, it can only mean that he's planning some sort of attack. I glance at Skye, knowing that we have to stop this meeting before it happens.

"Contact the plane," I tell Skye. "We're going to Tokyo."

Skye nods, tapping her earbuds. I turn away, looking down the hallway for any signs of more soldiers. Then Skye walks up to me, a concerned look on her face.

"August," she says.

I turn back to her, wondering what could be wrong.

"Something's happened," she continues. "The radio channel has been diverted to the base in California. They're saying to get out of here immediately." She pauses, listening to the radio chatter.

Skye then looks up at me. "The plane's been destroyed."

FOUR

Skye and I run back into the hallway, searching for the nearest exit to the base. The alarms blare all around. We emerge onto one of the outdoor walkways surrounding the base.

After we learned of the plane's destruction, NAIS High Command radioed us to discuss extraction. A chopper will meet us about two miles from our current position.

I hear the groan of a door opening behind us, and I whirl, unholstering my gun. Skye does the same, and we turn around to see a group of four enemy soldiers rushing toward us from across the bridge. I open fire. Two drop in rapid succession. Skye takes care of the other two, and we continue down the walkway, our pace quickening.

I push open the door at the end of the walkway, running inside to another hallway. As we round the corner of this one, I hear footsteps nearing us. A guard turns the corner, and as he does, I grab his arm and twist hard. I hear a bone snapping, and he shouts, flipping over and hitting the wall.

I run down a flight of stairs to a lower level, nearing the outskirts of the base. Skye nods toward a tall ridge lying in the distance. Beyond that is a small forest, and the chopper will meet us there at the riverbed.

We emerge onto a large platform that leads toward a long trail that winds out of the base. Something flashes in the corner of my eye, and I turn back in the way we came. A figure dressed in black armor jumps down from the roof, his face completely covered by a mask. He wields a pair of pistols, and I can spot two long daggers strapped to his back in a cross. He stands tall, and something about his nature makes him feel like a predator.

Before I can raise my gun, he opens fire on us. I raise my arms in a protective stance, tapping on my armguards. The braces expand into a circular metal shield, and the bullets clang against the hard metal. Skye rolls to the side, and a stream of bullets follows her as she ducks behind a stack of crates.

The armored figure lunges toward me, his pistols holstered and daggers out. He thrusts one of the blades towards me, and I avoid it, sweeping down under the strike. He thrusts a second time, and I raise my arm, the shield blocking the blade from striking my chest.

Skye dives onto him, swinging her leg up onto his neck. Her weight knocks his helmet sideways, and he falls to the ground with a grunt. I push myself up onto my feet and watch as Skye moves to knock him unconscious. The man turns onto his back, then pushes down on the ground with his hands and flips up onto his feet.

He raises a pistol this time, firing at Skye. I dive in front of her just in time, deflecting the bullets off my shield. He snarls, racing toward me with both daggers out. I pull my batons from my belt, parrying his oncoming strike. Skye pulls out a knife, running forward towards me. We attack him in sync, our moves a mix of thrusts and deflections. As Skye blocks his next attack, I find an opening, throwing one of my batons forward to knock him backward.

The man stumbles to the ground, his head turned upward towards us.

Before we can move forward to finish him, he stands up and dives off of the edge of the helipad. Skye and I exchange a glance, and as we rush to the edge, I watch as his armor expands into a set of wings. He maneuvers through the gorge below until he disappears from sight.

"Do you know who that was?" Skye asks me, strapping her knife back to her leg.

I shake my head. "No, but the suit he was using is highly advanced. I might have an idea of who created it for him."

Skye tilts her head at me, clearly asking to know.

"There was a man that used to work for the NAIS by the name of John Hayward. He designed advanced armor suits that were meant to be used for military combat. He disappeared several years ago, allegedly kidnapped."

Skye nods. "So that suit of armor, if Laurings has more of them, it could be a serious threat."

"When we get back to base, we'll inform the Director about it. Tracking down John Hayward should now be a top priority."

We continue down the pathway out of the base. The security is loose here, and we only come across several guards, which we take out with ease. Once we leave the base, we head down into a wide canyon, where a trail continues toward the woods.

The two of us keep moving like this until we're far beyond the base. I lead us up another pathway to where the ground levels back out to normal. To our left, I can spot an airstrip in the distance, where a jet is wheeling out onto the tarmac.

The sound of rotors whirring reaches my ears, and I turn my head up to see a sleek gray helicopter moving toward us, the NAIS insignia emblazoned on it as expected. It moves towards the woods, where our extraction point is.

I frown. The chopper is far too close to that airstrip—the pilot must not have known about it beforehand. I hear a loud siren noise coming from the airfield.

The turrets surrounding the base swivel in the direction of the chopper.

Skye sees this too, and my hand goes to my earbud, getting on the radio. "Chopper 13A, this is Commander Gilman. The turrets at the nearby airfield have focused on you—I repeat, you have incoming—"

I see a large explosion and then watch in horror as the entire helicopter goes up in flames overhead. The chopper swerves down towards the forest, crashing into a small clearing in a flurry of fire.

Skye rushes towards it, but I hold out a hand in front of her. "The soldiers at the airstrip will be heading to the wreckage to check for survivors. The chopper has just confirmed to them that we're still here," I tell her.

Skye nods. I know she understands.

We're both silent for a moment, and I realize that their deaths are partially our fault. They had come here to extract us, and it had cost them their lives. I glance at Skye, realizing how she must feel. This is her first time back in the field, and it only makes it worse that I'm the one who had asked her to come on the mission.

"Now's the time to move in," I tell Skye, pointing towards the airfield. "The security at the airfield will be less intense because some of the soldiers will be checking the wreckage."

"You're right." Skye seems more energized now. "It's possible that if we make it there, I can rewire one of the jets for takeoff. Can you still fly?"

I nod. "Let's get going."

After making our way across the outskirts of the base, Skye and I arrive at the airfield. I crouch on top of a ridge that overlooks the long strip of concrete. To the left lies a massive hangar with a steel roof, and I watch as a jet is directed out of the hangar's doors and onto the main airstrip.

Skye taps my shoulder, then points at a lone fighter jet being fueled up near the corner of the airfield. I nod back at her, and we make our way down the ridge toward it.

I watch in silence as a group of men dressed in black suits drag a long fuel pump across the airstrip to the fighter jet. I study the plane itself, noticing the text GOLD 2 emblazoned on the tail fin of the ship. The jet has a long curvature to it, the wings spread wine in a long arc. On each wing lies a heavy artillery gun alongside fin-mounted missile launchers. These planes are well-equipped and well-armed, and I wonder for a moment about where they must be heading.

I pull my pistol out of its holster, flipping a switch to silence the gun. I duck behind a tall boulder, and Skye skids down the path next to me, ready to attack. I hold up three fingers at Skye, who nods back. I slowly count to three in my head.

I emerge from the cover, side-stepping to the right side of the rocks. The soldiers fueling the planes shout as they spot us, but they don't manage to run five meters before we gun them down. I rush forward towards the plane, checking the fuel meter on the side of the hull. Seventeen thousand gallons should be enough to get us back to Tokyo. I nod at Skye, and she rushes to the security padlock that controls the plane's ability to take off.

I watch as she breaks open the metal box, revealing a set of colored wires tangled inside. Skye pulls a small pair of tweezers from her belt, and I back away as a small shower of sparks explodes from the padlock. I look around, searching for any sign of someone noticing us. When I see that the airfield is completely clear, I run to a small cutout in the airstrip, where I find a rack of weapons and ammunition. To the right of the rack is a tall ladder, and I pull it from its place towards the plane.

When I arrive back at the jet, I smile to see the cockpit already open, and the padlock closed. Skye nods, and I push the ladder up to the side of the jet.

Skye goes in first, and I follow her, moving into the pilot's seat at the front of the cockpit. Once we're settled into our seats, I flip a switch on the left console, and the cockpit's hatch closes.

My eyes survey the main consoles, and I find myself at ease in the cockpit. I learned to fly when I was twelve, and this space feels completely natural to me. I study the controls, realizing that they're luckily in English.

I turn a red knob, and the engine roars to life, the entire plane's body vibrating. I find the joystick near the center of the console and push it forward. The plane moves smoothly across the flat concrete, and my eyes narrow as a group of soldiers run across the tarmac toward us, waving their hands for me to stop the plane.

Ignoring them, I pull on the headset that lies on the armrest next to me. Static crackles through the radio before I hear a heavily-accented voice come through on the line.

"Gold 2, please return to your position. I repeat, Gold 2, please return to position 7," someone says through the radio.

When I don't reply, one of the soldiers coming towards the plane raises his gun and fires several warning shots. I ignore him, turning the plane down the airfield. I prep the engine for takeoff, then stop as I hear the clang of a bullet ricochet off of the plane's hull.

I jerk the joystick to the left, and the plane moves sharply in the direction of the soldiers. I press one of the buttons, and a targeting computer unfolds from the right console. I angle it so that it fits comfortably next to my head, and I pull a knob on the joystick. The weapons system comes online, and I continue turning the jet until the wing-mounted guns align directly with the oncoming soldiers. By the time they realize what's happening, it's too late.

I pull the trigger on the joystick, and a rush of bullets hits the soldiers. They go down in a matter of seconds, and I take my finger off of the trigger, letting the heavy guns cool down. I turn my attention to the center console, where I spot a red dot approaching our location. It's warning me that the turrets have locked onto our jet.

Veering the jet to the right at a sharp angle, I watch the console intently as a missile closes in. The only shot I have at avoiding it is if we manage to take off. I push the joystick forward hard, and the engines roar as we roll down the airstrip at an increasing speed. I pull a small lever to my right, and I hear the air flaps unfolding from the wing panels.

Once we reach a high enough speed, I pull the jet upwards into the air. The scraping of wheels against concrete disappears and is replaced by the sound of the wind roaring in my ears. The console beeps rapidly, warning me of the oncoming missile.

Skye leans forward from the backseat. "August," she tells me. "There's a missile coming for us."

I yank the headset off of my head, throwing it onto the ground. "I know," I shout over the heavy wind outside. "Turn on the ray shielding," I say. "The blue switch to your left. It'll protect us if we get hit."

Skye does it, and I watch the outer hull as a barely visible blue sheet slowly wraps around the exterior of the jet.

My seat vibrates, warning me of the incoming missile. I watch as a proximity bar to my right increases, reading ten meters before impact.

I turn the plane violently to the left, moving downwards in a long arc. Behind me, the missile swerves back in our direction. It's following us, confirming exactly what I'd feared. The turrets below are equipped with heat-seeking missiles.

My eyes move across the different consoles, searching for a purple switch. I find it next to the armrest, and it's labeled with the word FLARES. As the missile closes in on us, I push the switch. I watch as flaps on the wings open to fire brightly colored flares back in the direction of the missiles. One of them strikes true, and the entire plane shakes from the explosion behind us.

I hear Skye breathe a sigh of relief behind me, but I don't relax at all. I veer the jet to the left, turning at an angle that allows me to see the airfield below. I watch in dismay as two fighter jets roll out onto the runway and lift off toward us.

The main console beeps again, displaying two more missiles headed toward us. I pull the control yokes back as far as I can, and the nose of the jet turns upwards at the cloudy sky. I turn a knob, which diverts the main power to the engines. The rear thrusters roar, and the entire jet rockets skyward.

Down below, the other fighter jets pursue us high into the air. I use the thick clouds as a veil, trying to throw the oncoming planes off. The proximity meter lights up, and I realize that the newly launched missiles have gotten much closer. I pull on the flare switch again, but it glows red. Because I'm diverting so much power to the engines, there's not enough energy to launch the flares.

I swerve to the right, and the missiles turn to follow me. I push the yokes all the way to the left, and the jet turns so that the nose is facing the oncoming missiles. I open fire, and a round of heavy bullets bursts out at the warheads. The first missile explodes, taking the second one with it.

The hull shudders around me as one of the fighter jets closes in on us, its heavy guns deployed and firing a stream of bullets. I hear the shields around us shudder, slowly breaking apart from the oncoming fire.

I turn the nose of the jet all the way downwards so that the tip of the jet is pointed directly at the ground, the body of the plane perpendicular to the earth. I push forward hard on the acceleration meter, and the engines roar as the jet moves toward the ground. We cut through the clouds, and below lies a wide canyon. Behind us, I hear the intensity of the bullets increase, and I spin hard to the right, trying to avoid taking more damage.

The console beeps in front of me, warning me against impact with the ground. I look forward beyond the cockpit's canopy, suddenly realizing how close we've gotten to the earth. At the last second, I pull up on the control yokes, the tip of the jet barely leveling out in time. I hear one of the rear thrusters scrape against the ground and break off in the process, but I ignore this and pull back on the acceleration.

The jet slows down to a more reasonable speed, and I have to maneuver around the massive rock structures littering the canyon. Behind us, I hear the two enemy jets pulling up behind us, getting a higher vantage point above the canyon. My eyes narrow—these pilots know what they're doing, and I'll have to pull off something unexpected to take them down.

I pull back on the yokes as hard as I can, and the jet's nose turns upward. We soar upwards, our backs towards the ground. The two jets split behind us, and I head towards the one on the left.

It opens fire on us, and I swerve left, leading it down into the canyon. It follows me, precisely what I had hoped. Our jet narrowly makes it through a small crevice in between two cliff faces, and the other one follows. Right as we make it through, I turn the jet towards the opening. Before the other pilot can react, I fire three missiles directly into the oncoming fighter. The jet doesn't even make it through the hole before it bursts into flames.

Our jet is pushed back from the impact into the open canyon. The other remaining jet swerves towards us, taking advantage of the lack of cover around us right now. I push on the acceleration lever as hard as I can, but the engines sputter in return. The explosion must have damaged the central exhaust unit.

My muscles tense as I hear the oncoming fighter deploy a missile.

"Bail out!" I shout to Skye.

She nods at me and pulls on the crank next to her seat. She launches out into the sky, her parachute deploying. I wait for several seconds, waiting for the jet to be directly above our stuck position. Now.

I do the same, and as I pull the lever, I'm thrown upwards, narrowly avoiding the jet as it roars past. I pull my knife from my belt and tear through the parachute. I fall downwards, landing on the back end of the fighter jet. I grab onto a small handle usually used for fueling the plane, which stops me from sliding. I hang on to the back of the jet as the pilot pulls up at a slight slant.

The jet shakes as an explosion sounds from behind, the result of the missile destroying the other fighter jet. I grab onto a hold behind the cockpit, slowly edging forward along the hull of the plane without the pilot noticing. I'm lucky that he's keeping the jet level for now.

When I reach the cockpit, I press my body against the hull of the jet to stay out of the pilot's range of sight. We're still low to the ground, but I feel the wind picking up as he tilts the jet upwards. I unholster my gun, pressing the barrel against the hinge at the back of the cockpit. If I blow off the wires, the canopy will loosen.

I fire, and the back of the cockpit explodes in sparks. The pilot turns his head, and as he does, the front of the cockpit's canopy slowly lifts up. I pull myself further up across the body of the plane, and as the pilot looks behind him, I send a bullet into his skull.

His body slacks, and I climb into the cockpit, pushing his body aside and overboard. I pull the canopy back over my head, locking it back into place. I glance at the broken hinge that kept it in place. The canopy won't stay in place for long— we'll have to find a way to weld the hinge back into place.

I turn the jet, heading back in the direction of where Skye ejected from the original jet. She waves at me from a ridge around fifty meters away, seemingly aware of what happened. I smile. She knew exactly what I was planning.

The jet touches down on the ridge where Skye is, the landing gear unfolding onto the rocky ground. I pull open the canopy, and Skye pulls herself onto the wing, then settles into the cockpit behind me.

"You good?" she asks, strapping herself in.

"Yeah, I'm fine," I reply. "But I had to shoot the hinge holding the canopy in place. Is there any way you could manage to fix it?"

Skye frowns, twisting to take a good look at the broken hinge behind her. She studies it for several seconds, eyeing the torn wires.

"I think I could work something out," Skye says. "How far do we need to go?"

I think about this for a moment, remembering that the arms dealing was in Tokyo. I recall an NAIS outpost in the city, and if we could get there, they could resupply us for the next mission.

"Could we make it to Tokyo?" I ask her.

She seems to contemplate that. "I think so," Skye answers. "Though, do we have enough fuel to make that trip?"

I glance at the fuel meter to my right. I burned a lot of fuel during that chase, though there should be enough left for us to make it to Japan. I nod at Skye.

"Alright, then." Skye pulls a small welding torch from her belt and nods back.

I stand up, pulling the canopy down back into place. I push the control yokes forward, and the jet lifts off the ridge and into the air. The landing gear folds up into the hull, and the air flaps extend outward. I pull up the map on the console, plotting a course to reach Tokyo.

We're on our way to Laurings.

FIVE

It's been several hours since we left the Alps. Outside, the sky is dark, but there are stars everywhere. They are bright white, unaffected by artificial light coming from nearby cities. I watch as the moon rises on the horizon, and when I shift to the side and look to the ground, I see rolling sand dunes transitioning into a series of marshes. We must be somewhere in Africa—the desert leading into the plains is a sure sign.

"Why didn't you tell me you were shot?"

She grimaces, swallowing. "I didn't want to bother you," she replies, teeth gritted through the pain. "I figured you had enough on your hands."

I pull a knob, and the plane starts to fly itself.

"Come on, Skye, you know that you're supposed to tell me about this stuff. Don't hide it."

I hand her a fresh roll of bandages, and she wraps them tightly around the wound.

"Thanks," Skye says.

We both settle into silence, and I turn back into my seat, keeping my eyes on the air space ahead. I move the throttle forward—I want to get her medical help as soon as possible, and we have enough, just enough, fuel to do it.

I let the sounds of the easy wind outside the cockpit relax me as I steer our jet through the clouds. Skye fell asleep an hour ago, and I still keep an eye on her, making sure that her wound isn't worsening.

The console beeps a single time, indicating that we're nearing our destination. As I glance outside of the canopy, I spot the first signs of land peering through the thick fog. This is the island of Honshu, home of the Japanese capital.

A couple of hours later, we pass the famous Mount Fuji, the tallest peak in Japan. It's a beautiful mountain stretching for miles in either direction and at its height lies the open mouth of a volcano. But up ahead is the real marvel.

I slow the jet down so that I can get a better view of the city below. Tokyo is a sprawling metropolis, its buildings spiraling thousands of feet into the air. Spectacular neon lights illuminate every billboard, alley, and street light, covering the city in a bright hue. Monorail tracks weave in between the buildings much higher up in the air, seemingly held up by slanted metal columns. My eyes wander towards the outskirts of the city, where large planes are taking off and setting down at a massive airport lit with golden light.

Skye stirs behind me. She gazes out the window, her eyes reflecting the bright lights of the city.

She then turns toward me and asks, "This is Tokyo, right? It's beautiful."

I nod. "The agency's building will be further inside the city."

We fall into an awe-filled silence, our eyes set on the expansive city below us. I keep the jet up high in the clouds, away from any satellite detection. The NAIS has something similar to an embassy within Tokyo, and if I recall correctly, we're getting fairly close to it. I pull my earbuds from their case, fitting them in my ears. I change the channel to 17.

A voice comes through. "Agent, please identify yourself. This is a heavily protected channel. I repeat, please identify yourself."

"This is Agent August Gilman of Base 13 in Yosemite," I reply. "We were rerouted from a mission in the Alps to this base."

Static crackles through the radio. "Agent Gilman, register your chain code."

A chain code is a unique pattern of letters and numbers used to identify agents. Every time an agent requests permission to land at a base, they must authorize the chain code in order to enter.

"134 - 4RF - 7UJ."

I wait in silence for several seconds.

"Agent Gilman, your chain code has been confirmed. We will contact the Japanese embassy, and your jet will be authorized to land at Pad 14 in the Central City. From there, we'll send a car to bring you to the American embassy. Have a safe landing."

The channel turns off. I start a slow descent toward the ground, careful to avoid the monorail tracks and the lit paths that the cars take to float through the city.

Near the center of the city, a towering skyscraper looms over the rest of the buildings around it. This must be the Japanese embassy. Landing pads extend from its levels, where other vehicles are landing as well. Each pad is lit with a number, and I search for 14. I see the number on one of the upper-level pads, and I slowly set the jet down on it.

As the jet sets down, a man flanked on either side by guards emerges from a large archway leading onto the pad. I lift up the canopy and help Skye climb out. The bandages that we've strapped around the bullet wound are clotted with blood, and Skye has to lean heavily on my shoulder, keeping her weight on her good leg.

My attention returns to the man who's come to greet us. I study him, noticing his slicked-back hair and tall posture. He's older, maybe in his fifties. He must be who represents the NAIS at Tokyo's central landing hub.

"Agent Gilman," he says, crossing the landing pad to greet us. He extends a hand to me, and I shake it. He then turns to Skye and addresses her as just "Skye". I narrow my eyes. Maybe they've met before.

At the entrance to the landing pad, two soldiers reel out a long stretcher. Because we alerted them in advance that Skye was wounded, their medical staff is ready to treat her. Skye climbs onto the stretcher, and they carry her towards the archway that leads off of the suspended pad.

"Welcome to Tokyo," the man says. "If you follow me, I'll take you to the front lot. The NAIS has sent a car for you."

We follow him back through the archway and into a large elevator. Once we reach the ground floor, the man leads us out into a parking lot. A sleek black car drives in through the gates, stopping at the curb to let us in. Its door slides open, and I help Skye off of her stretcher and into the car. I climb into the front seat next to the operator, and two of the soldiers follow us into the large vehicle, tasked with the job of keeping us safe until we reach the American embassy. Additionally, a woman dressed in a doctor's lab coat boards with us, most likely to make sure that Skye's wound doesn't get worse.

The car turns into a line of traffic, and I glance outside the heavily tinted windows of the car, studying the breathtaking technology of this city. Each skyscraper outside of the airways has exteriors completely constructed of strong glass, a material that is resistant to bullets. Bright lights of all colors hang from tall billboards on the sides of buildings, and the same airways that we're in now are present across the entire city. Metal walkways extend between towering buildings high in the air, and people walk across them, completely unafraid of the length of the drop to the ground levels of the city.

We begin to head toward a complex of buildings. These structures are close to the center of the city and are neither high in the sky nor close to the ground. The car drives past a squadron of hovering drones, and I realize they are all equipped with heavy-mounted turrets. Security is tight here, so we must be nearing the American embassy.

Behind me, Skye groans in pain, and I hear the shuffling of equipment as the soldiers clear the back space for the doctor to take a look at her. I shift in my seat and press a button with a rotating symbol on it. The chair spins around and turns to face Skye.

"The bullet nearly missed one of her major arteries," the doctor tells me, pulling her glasses on.

She leans in closer to Skye to inspect her leg, and I swallow as I realize that blood is flowing rapidly from the bullet wound.

"We need to get to the treatment room now," the doctor says to the operator, and he nods at her. "She's losing a lot of blood."

Keeping an eye on Skye, I'm thrown back in my seat as the car starts to move at an increased rate. The car surges forward on the concrete road, and I hear the engine shut off as we pull to a stop.

The doctor nods at me, and I open the door. The two soldiers lift Skye back onto the stretcher and carry her out onto another landing platform. My eyes survey the building in front of us. It's another spectacle of architecture, designed with the base colors of white and gray, with gold highlighting the building's arches and bows. In the center of the building's main face is a large plaque with the American and Japanese flags emblazoned on it. A sign reads AMERICAN EMBASSY.

We're led in through the front double doors by a group of guards. From here, we cross the lobby and into a separate wing of the embassy. We board a large glass elevator that leads up into the building. Finally, we emerge into an expansive room lit by golden light. In the center of the cavernous space lies a statue of an eagle—the symbol of the NAIS.

Skye is taken into a separate room for medical treatment, and I find myself pacing in the corner of the room. The man who led us here in the first place approaches me.

"She'll be fine," he tells me. His English is crisp and clear.

"That's great," I tell him, staring out the glass windows at the glowing city that surrounds this building. "Did our commander send you our new orders?" I ask.

The man nods. "She wants you to debrief us first before we inform you on the mission. She also says that she sent someone to assist you, someone that you know. If you follow me, we can get started."

I follow the man up a spiral staircase onto an open-air balcony, wondering who this person he mentioned could be. Here, he leads me to a table in the center of the balcony where a diagram of the city is now displayed. He gives a nod to the guards, and they exit the rooftop. Clearly, the information I have is classified.

My eyes move back to the round table in front of me. I realize that this city is actually much larger than I thought. The skyscrapers extend for miles in every direction, leading toward the mountains surrounding the city.

The man steps closer to me, and he nods at me. "So, August, tell me about your mission. Anything worth noting?"

"We have Laurings' location now. It's here in Tokyo."

I study the man's face. He already knew this because why else would we come here rather than turning back to the states?

"He's meeting with an arms dealer for some kind of exchange later this week. At a place in the central city called Hades Plaza. Skye believes that the particular building that they're meeting in is called Royce Tower."

The man pulls out a tablet on which he enters this information. Likely sending the data to the briefing room for them to prepare for the mission. "Is there anything else?"

"Yeah," I say. "We were attacked by someone in an advanced combat suit on our way out of the base. It was bullet resistant and had a parachute built into its armor."

"Thank you for the information. If you follow me, I'll take you to the agent Taylor sent for you."

He leads me back down into the embassy, where he takes us into a wide, circular room. At the opposite end of the space is a young man studying a set of pistols on a table in front of him.

"Hunter?" I say, moving across the room towards him.

As I speak, he stands up, a grin breaking across his face. "August."

Hunter stands and walks to me. He extends his hand, and I shake it. He looks exactly the same as I remember from several months ago - high cheekbones, thin eyebrows, and straight, neat brown hair.

Hunter is another agent in the NAIS; I've known him since childhood. We trained together during apprenticing, and he was my old partner before I met Skye. Hunter is an extremely talented field agent; he specializes in fast, precise operations, the perfect skill set for the mission that we're about to undergo.

"Is Skye alright?" Hunter asks me. "I heard she was shot."

I think they're performing surgery on her now. The doctor said she'd be fine. Did Taylor send you?"

"She did. I'm here to back you up for the mission."

"Good." I turn back to the man who led us to the embassy. "Can you brief us on the mission?"

"Follow me," he says, leading us into a hallway.

We enter another circular room. Grouped at stations, I see analysts and other agents. In the center of the room is a massive hologram-like screen, on which is displayed a large section of the central city. The group of buildings is made up of seven large skyscrapers and a hotel building. This must be Hades Plaza.

The largest skyscraper to the left is highlighted in a red glow. I assume this is Royce Tower, the place where Laurings is meeting the arms dealers. I study the building, starting from the ground level. It looks like the entire base of the tower has large brick walls surrounding it, with guards patrolling each side of it in rotations. On the inside of the large walls, a driveway leads into the building, where security is equally as tight. Each panel of the exterior glass windows on the skyscraper is tinted dark black, likely one-way bulletproof glass. Each level has office spaces and meeting lounges, but the one floor that sticks out to me is the sixty-seventh. There, a group of drones circles the exterior paneling. Not only that but a small, barely visible barbed wire fence extends along the four sides of the skyscraper on that level. This is, without doubt, where Laurings is going to be making the exchange.

I point at this floor, and the rest of the people in the room gather near me, studying the detailed diagram with me.

"Laurings is going to be meeting with the representatives from Leonard Industries here."

One of the analysts steps forward beside me.

"I agree," she says. "The security is excessive there, especially with the fencing around it. Our objective will be to reach that floor and get a shot at Laurings, if possible. We will have agents with thermal-scoped rifles gathered on the buildings surrounding Royce Tower. At the very least, we have to stop the arms exchange between Laurings and that group."

"Hunter, Skye, and I are going to be entering the building?" I ask her.

"Yes," the analyst replies. "You three will be accompanied by two other experienced field agents. However, access to that building is extremely limited.

We haven't had enough time to find a way in with permission from the building's lobby. This operation is going to require your group to enter the building through the side entrance, where you'll have to take down several guards on arrival. We're currently dispatching satellites to scramble the building's radio chatter, so you should have around fifteen minutes to make it to the sixty-seventh before the alarm sounds," she finishes.

I swallow, in awe of how quickly these analysts have formulated a plan to enter the skyscraper. They're damn good at their job.

Hunter crosses the room to stand next to me. "So if all goes well, we're going to eliminate the guards at the west entrance and attempt to make it onto the elevator leading up to floor sixty-seven. Do you have any evidence that we'll be able to access that elevator?" He seems to be on edge about this entire mission.

The analyst nods at him. "We've taken a highly precise satellite scan, and the keycards that the guards carry will all give access to the elevators. From there, you'll be able to reach Laurings' level and hopefully take a shot at him. You'll all be equipped with hyper light gliders to make an escape off of the building, and to break the glass, we'll arm you with detonators."

I take in this plan, noting how risky it is, how many things can go wrong. But if the intel we got from the Alps is correct, then stopping this arms dealing is a top priority right now. Laurings could be planning some sort of nuclear launch on the NAIS.

"According to August and Skye's intel, the deal will be made tomorrow at midnight," another analyst tells us. "For now, you'll get rest and be equipped with the necessary weapons and gear for the upcoming operation."

The crowd in the room disperses, and Hunter and I follow an officer to the rooms we'll be staying in for the night. I collapse onto the large bed, changing into a fresh set of clothes from my jumpsuit.

I stretch my arms, my muscles sore from a long day. Outside, the beautiful city of Tokyo is still brightly lit in the dark night.

I feel myself falling asleep in the quietness, but I sit up at the sound of a rap against the window. When the sound comes again, I swing my legs over the side of the bed, standing up on the carpet. I reach under the dresser where I left my gun. I hold it up at the window, eerily suspicious. When nothing more comes, my shoulders slump back, and I turn to place the gun back in its place.

The wide window shatters open, and glass flies in toward me. I gasp in pain as one of the shards catches me hard in the shoulder, and I fall backward onto the ground. A figure dressed in a black suit swings into the room, a gun in their hand. It takes me a moment to realize that it's the same man from the base in the Alps. His face is still shrouded in a black mask.

I dive behind the bed as he fires a clip of bullets at me. All around, different walls, lamps, and shelves are torn to pieces as the suited man fires on me. My eyes search the room frantically, trying to find where my gun went. I see it across the large space tucked under a tall clock structure. It must have been knocked out of my hand after the window shattered.

I tap my wristband, and it expands into a metal shield once again. I rise from my place behind the bed, holding up the shield and running for the gun. The man turns his gun towards me, perfectly tracking me as I rush across the room. The bullets ricochet off of the shield, and I lunge for the gun, grabbing it as I roll behind a wall.

My breaths come in heavy gasps, and I press my back against the wall. I check my bullet chamber. Only two left. I must have forgotten to reload it since the last time I used it. I duck as a fresh round of bullets puts holes into the wall behind me. A glass vase above my head shatters, and I dash to the left into the bathroom. The man's footsteps grow closer, and I look around the bathroom, searching for anything I can use. I see the man's silhouette round the corner, and as he walks through, I fire my last two bullets at the pipes running along the ceiling. They crack open, and a stream of water bursts into the man. The force knocks him back, and I lunge at him, my leg up. I knock him back into the opposite wall and throw my fist into his mask. The punch goes through, and part of the mask breaks open. I feel my knuckles collide with his jawbone, and the man shouts in return.

He throws his own fist into my stomach, and I collapse back into the main section of the room once more. The man grabs his gun from where it fell on the floor and fires another round at me. I raise my arm, the shield deflecting the bullets. His armored figure steps closer to me, and I back up against the bed. He pulls a fresh clip of bullets from his belt and reloads his gun. As he does, I take the opportunity to attack.

I kick my leg out at his ankle and catch him right in the joint. His leg buckles and he falls forward. I snake towards him, wrapping my leg around his neck in a chokehold. He grabs my leg with his arm, trying to throw me off of him. The man gasps for air and throws his head back into my chest. The quick movement knocks the breath out of me, and in my pain, I release my hold on him. He rises to his feet, and I spring into a standing position as well. He snarls, dashing towards me. The man throws his shoulder into mine, and pain lances through my entire body. I collapse backward to the edge of the room where the window was shattered, taking the man with me. The force of his charge sends me skidding over the smooth marble floor, and I slide over the edge of the building. At the last moment, I'm able to grip onto the steel skeleton of the broken window, and I feel the rest of my body dangle over the edge.

It takes me a second to realize that the man who attacked me is no longer on me. I pull myself up and over the edge of the building, my muscles burning. I look out over the outline of the city outside, the cold breeze making a loud whistling noise.

I spot a black silhouette gliding through the air in between a set of buildings. I sigh in relief, realizing that he must have been thrown off of the side of the building with me. But his suit must still have that glider built into it. That confirms that he was the one who attacked Skye and me earlier at Laurings' base in Europe.

Behind me, I hear a group of guards rushing into the room, their guns raised. The commotion must have drawn them here. One of them approaches me, helping me to my feet.

"What happened, sir?"

I struggle to my feet, and the guard helps me onto the bed.

"I was attacked. The same man that came at Skye and me in the Alps. He came in through the window, wearing the same suit and mask that I remember." I turn towards the guard. "They knew I was here, at the embassy, in this room. Somebody wants me dead."

The man shouts to another soldier to get a medic for me. He motions to a senior officer. The two of them exchange a glance with each other before exiting the room, leaving the other guards as security for me.

Without saying it, I have implied something very dangerous. They're going to check the security footage of the exterior building, and when they see that I'm telling the truth, the entire embassy will have to be put on lockdown. Someone who knew my whereabouts leaked this out and tried to have me killed.

There is a traitor among us.

SIX

The guards take me into another guest room on the floor above my old room. I have them stay stationed at the door throughout the night. I stay awake for several long hours, my hand constantly resting on the gun that lies on my bedside desk. And when I do eventually fall asleep, it's a fitful one, full of nightmares of gunshots and blood.

I wake up late in the morning the next day. Bright sunlight flows in through the closed curtains, and I swing my legs over the side of the bed. I head into the shower, the warm water soothing my sore muscles. I change into a new jumpsuit, fitting my gun into the holster at my side.

I pull open the door to my room and head out into the hallway. The two guards on either side of the doorway give me a nod, each holding a machine gun in their hands. One of them accompanies me, and we head down to the main floor, where the rest of the agents are already most likely gearing up for the mission later today.

The elevator doors slide open, and I step out of the elevator into a massive circular room where people are milling about. In the corner of the space, the two other agents, aside from Hunter and Skye, are being outfitted with weaponry. I see Hunter making his way across the room as well, seemingly with a slight limp on his right leg. I narrow my eyes, wondering if he's alright.

My eyes land on Skye, who is studying a hologram in the center of the room. I walk over to her. As I near her, she turns in her seated position towards me and smiles.

"Hey, Skye," I say. "Holding up okay?"

She nods at me. "The surgery went well. I think they got the bullet out really quickly, and someone told me I should be good for the mission, so long as I keep this brace on," Skye replies.

She gestures to a long cylindrical metal piece that is stretched around the area of her leg where she was hit by the bullet.

"August, I heard you were attacked last night in your room." She looks up at me. "The same person as at the base in the Alps?"

"Same exact armor, same style of movement. Whoever they are, they want me dead badly, and they know where I am."

"Well, they have the embassy on lockdown," Skye says in a reassuring tone. "They'll find whoever it is eventually. For now, we just gear up for the mission ahead of us and hope for the best."

I nod at her. "Alright, I'll see you at mission time."

The hours pass by quickly. As darkness falls outside, our group does a weapons and ammunitions check before we leave. Once we make sure that we're geared up, the guards lead us out a side entrance of the embassy and into a heavily shielded military car. The vehicle takes us through the city and toward the plaza where Laurings is meeting the arms company for the exchange.

Once we arrive, we exit the car in a narrow alleyway near the plaza. The two other agents, experienced veterans that have done missions like this before, lead us through the lowest levels of the city towards the plaza. I keep my heavy rifle strapped across my back, covering it with a cloak that I wear.

As we approach the plaza, we keep behind the towering buildings, using the shadows to mask our movement. To the left lies Royce Tower, a massive structure paneled with clear glass. A large gate circles the skyscraper, just as I saw in the mission briefing. Guards surround the entire perimeter, and bright white light shines down from places along the outer fencing.

I signal to the group to continue moving forward. We work our way around to the left side of the tower, moving across the plaza. When we draw closer to Royce Tower, I unclip my cloak from my back and leave it on the ground. I pull my rifle from my back, and the others do the same.

I crouch behind a small fountain to the left of the west gate. The gate structure itself lies almost twenty meters away from my current position. A total of three guards stand at this area of the gate, all of them alert with their guns out. Skye is crouched next to me. Hunter and the other two agents are around fifteen meters to our left. They'll create a distraction while Skye and I take the guards out from behind.

I tap my earbud and give Hunter a quiet go ahead. I hear a single gunshot sound out to the left, and the guards startle, their shouts going up. I switch my channel and then tell the analysts to block the satellite's signals.

As the guards at the gate pull out their radios, their expressions turn confused as they realize they can't call for help. Another gunshot comes from Hunter's position, and the guards raise their guns and move slowly toward the building in which Hunter and the others are waiting.

As they do, Skye and I emerge from behind the fountain and open fire on the guards. They go down before even having a chance to shout out. I turn over one of their bodies and take the keycard that the guard was holding.

Hunter and the other two agents meet us at the gate. We stay away from the bright lights that shine down from the top of the gate, sticking to the shadows. I fire a single shot at the security camera that hangs down on the side of the gate's wire. Sparks fly from it, and it turns downwards, its connection sheared.

Now with the security down, I'm able to work on getting through the fence. I pull a small circular device from my belt and place it on the solid brick section of the gate. I tap it once, and its surface glows red. We back away from the gate.

I watch as a ring of teeth expands from the device and wrap around the face of the gate. A small hiss comes from it, and the concrete of the wall slowly starts to break away. After barely thirty seconds, the wall has bent and broken down, creating a large hole in the gate. I nod at the others and motion for them to go through the hole. I keep an eye out at the dark plaza around us, making sure everything is clear. Once they've all gone through, I duck down and slide through the hole in the gate and make my way onto the other side.

The concrete lot inside the gate is dark and largely unsupervised. I can spot a single guard making a rotation across the space, and I duck down further into the shadows, leading the others toward the west entrance. A door with a large padlock on it lies on this side of the building, and when we reach it, I slide the keycard I got from the guard from earlier across the scanner. It blinks green and unlocks.

I step inside the building into a maintenance hallway. I raise my gun, checking to make sure there's no one here. I shoot the security camera and then start heading down the hall, leading the others in behind me.

The hallway ends at a side entrance to the main lobby of the tower, and through the grated window, I can see a large group of guards welcoming in a group of people. I watch as they're escorted into the elevators at the end of the lobby.

"I count nine guards," I whisper quietly to the other agents, fitting a silencing extension onto my pistol. "They're currently taking a group of guests into the elevators. As they do, my guess is that some of them will accompany the guests while the others remain in the lobby. We're going to move in a protective unit and take them out as quickly as possible—silencers on. From there, we'll move into the elevators and up to the sixty-seventh floor. Understood?"

The group nods at me. Inside the lobby, the guards have taken the guests into the elevator. As I had assumed, six of them have stayed behind in the lobby. I hold up three of my fingers, then slowly count down.

As I finish counting down from three, I turn the handle of the door and push it open. I tap the band on my wrist, and the device expands into a metal shield. I rush through the entrance, and the others follow. The guards look up at us and shout from the other end of the lobby space. I raise my gun and fire, taking one of them down.

Bullets soar back and forth down the open space, and I hold up my shield, moving to position it against the oncoming fire. I duck down behind the concierge's desk, who is cowering under the table with their hands on their head. I see Skye take down two of the guards as well, and I continue to return fire at the guards. Within seconds, all of them are dead. I survey our group, making sure no one is injured.

Several more bullets ring out as Skye fires on the security cameras in the room. I run across the lobby to the back wall, where a large access panel is. I pull my knife from my belt and cut open the metal box, unveiling the wires and chords running inside of it. One of the other agents hands me a flash drive, and I plug it into a port within the panel. The drive will give the embassy access to the security systems of the building, but only for ten minutes.

Skye jogs up to me, giving me a nod that she's ready to go up to Laurings' floor. Hunter and the others follow me to the elevator, and I signal the embassy to send an elevator down for us. We need control of the security systems to access the elevators. They require keycards that we don't currently have.

The elevator rings as it arrives. Its sleek metal doors slide open, and we step inside, the doors closing behind us. My earbud vibrates in my ear, and I tap it once, wondering what could be wrong.

"Agent Gilman," one of the analysts says through the radio. "The security system has blocked our access to the sixty-seventh floor. There seems to be some sort of firewall restricting us from sending your elevator there. We can send you up to Floor Sixty, but after that, you and the others will have to free-climb through the shafts. Affirmative?"

I swallow, glancing at my watch. Nine minutes before the building will get control of their radios and security system. We have to do this as efficiently as possible.

"Affirmative," I reply through the earbud. "Send us to Floor Sixty, and we'll do the rest."

I tap the earbud again, and it switches off. The other agents look to me, and I tell them about the new plan. It's a bump in the road, but if we work quickly, we can still break up this arms deal.

I feel the elevator begin to move upwards, and the number on the glass panel in front of me increases as we go up the levels. After barely thirty seconds, the elevator rings out, signaling that we've made it to Floor Sixty. That's as far as we can go.

I move to the center of the elevator, then crane my neck upwards to get a good view at the top panel of the elevator, where we'll be getting into the shafts. I cut the hatch open with my knife, and I nod at the others to go up before me. Once they've all pulled themselves up into the shafts, Skye extends a hand down through the top to me. I grab the sides of the top panel and pull myself through.

The five of us crouch on top of the elevator in the dark shafts. The space is dusty and old, with cobwebs hanging on the walls. The four cables that pull the elevator cars are in each of the corners, and I look around for the maintenance ladder. I spot it on the left side, and I move across the elevator's top towards it.

As I do, the elevator below me shakes and begins to move downward. I jump forward and grab onto a sturdy metal pipe, setting my feet on a ledge below me.

"Grab hold of something!" I shout to the others, and they do the same as me, securing a hand on one of the various holds in the shaft.

The elevator moves downwards, dropping all the way back to the ground. I turn my eyes away from the shaft below, now hundreds of feet deep.

I glance at my watch. Seven minutes until the security is back online. I pull myself up onto the maintenance ladder, a strong tower of metal grips stretching upwards hundreds of times. I gesture for the others to work their way around the shaft to me, and I begin heaving myself upwards towards the sixty-seventh floor.

I'm nearly there when I hear the whir of an elevator car moving up towards us. I signal to the others and move up at an accelerated pace. Hunter, who is on the lowest rung of the ladder below, is forced to jump lightly onto the elevator car's roof. Skye, myself, and the others do the same, jumping down onto the car.

I narrow my eyes, searching through the grated roof of the elevator for the people inside. Two burly men holding machine guns are flanking a rack of tube-shaped objects. I study the pointed ends before I realize that I'm staring down at a set of warheads. The others see this, too, and I hold a finger to my lips, reminding them to stay silent.

The elevator continues upwards until it reaches the sixty-seventh floor. The men in the elevator, likely working for the arms dealer, step out through the elevator's doors. The doors slide close as they exit.

I crouch further down onto the roof of the elevator, and I gently lift the top access panel and move it aside. I unholster my gun and fit a silencer on it. Through the grates, I can make out the shape of the security camera in the corner, and I shoot it out. Making sure that the entire elevator is clear, I slowly lower myself down inside. The others follow me in.

I tap the button to open the elevator's doors, and they slide open, revealing a long hallway. Two guards stand on either side of the elevator's exit, and I react quickly. I pull my knife from my belt and cut one across the throat. Hunter does the same.

I catch my guard's body before it hits the ground and look for anywhere to hide it. I pull open a small closet in the hallway, and Hunter and I push the bodies inside and lock its doors. Skye and Hunter make their way across the hallway to the end, where they stand guard. One of the other two agents places a small orb next to the elevator, a small camera that will warn us if more soldiers are coming up through the elevator.

Once they're finished, our group approaches the end of the hallway, where a tall wooden door leads into the main space of this floor. I nod at Skye, who opens it slowly.

We emerge into a small lobby area, clearly intended for some sort of security purpose. The single guard standing inside doesn't even have a chance to raise his weapon before I knock him out with several well-placed hits with my fists. I check my watch, realizing that there are only two minutes before the security is back. We have no time to hide this body.

I continue towards the main space. I can hear voices coming from around the corner of this lobby room. Some of the details, I can't catch, but many of them come through clearly. They're discussing prices and locations, by the sounds of it.

I nod at the same agent who placed the security orb earlier. She takes another one of them and places it on the ground, getting us an angle of the meeting room itself. She then hands me a small tablet on which is displayed the camera's view.

There's an open space on the screen, surrounded on three sides by floor-to-ceiling glass windows. A set of three long tables are set up in the center of the area, with racks of explosives and weapons laid out on top of them. To the left stands a group of seven men dressed in heavily armored suits and carrying guns. Three of them hold shining silver cases in their hands. The payment.

On the right side stand the arms dealers. Six. Each one with heavy weaponry. Both of the groups seem relaxed, as though they've met each other before just like this.

But the groups of soldiers on either side of the room aren't what interests me. What does are the two men standing in the center of the room, who are engaged in conversation. The arms dealer is a tall man, built strong with wide shoulders. He is showing off one of the explosives to the other man, who I know the name of without a second thought.

This is our chance to kill Laurings.

SEVEN

"I have eyes on Laurings," I whisper to Skye. "I'm going to take a shot at him."

She nods.

"When they position themselves against us, you lead the others through the escape plan. I'll follow once you're all out."

Skye moves to tell the other agents the updated plan. I unholster my pistol, preparing to take my shot at Laurings. We won't have another good chance at taking him out. My bullets have to hit him clean, two in the chest and one in the head.

I nod again to the rest of the agents, who ready their gliders. Hunter moves to the back end of the hallway. He's making sure there's no one coming through the elevators. I hold up three fingers and slowly count down.

I sprint out from behind the lobby area, my gun up, firing. One of Laurings' soldiers pushes him to the ground. My shots instead strike the soldier, and he falls to the ground, dead.

I turn my gun towards the arms dealer and fire. Both of my bullets strike him in the head. The guards scramble and raise their guns at me to return fire. I flip the nearest table on its side and duck behind it for cover.

A hundred different scenarios pass through my head. How could Laurings' men know I was there at that exact time? Was it sheer luck that they saw me just in time to protect Laurings? Something simply isn't adding up.

I shout to Skye and the others to tell them to blow the windows. A small explosion sounds as Skye heaves a heavy grenade at the windows behind me. The glass shatters, and the wind whistles as a breeze floods into the room. More gunfire erupts, and I motion for the others to go. The two other agents jump through the open side of the building, deploying their parachutes as they go.

Hunter runs towards me, keeping his head down. His arm has a bloody streak running down it, a cut, or a bullet wound.

"They shot my parachute!" he shouts, ducking next to me behind the table. "If I jump, it won't deploy!"

I swallow, moving to get a look at his parachute. He's right; the fabric is cut and torn. If he jumps, the chute won't catch any wind.

"What are you going to do?" I ask. "I can't just leave you here!"

A pained look spreads across his face, and he glances behind him. I shuffle in my crouch, moving away from the holes ripping through the table.

"I'll try to get out through the elevator. Go, and I'll try to meet you back at the embassy."

I nod, then turn towards the open window. I know I'm going to regret leaving Hunter behind, but there's nothing I can do for him right now.

I build up momentum and jump through the cracked frame of glass. I fall out into the open air, the cityscape lit with neon light as I plummet down towards the ground. My hand goes to the tab on my back, and I pull it. My arms are pulled outwards as a black chute expands from the device on my back. Metal chords run across the fabric on the chute, slowing my descent. Ahead and to the left of me,

Skye and the other agents are gliding between two skyscrapers. I angle myself towards them and follow their path.

Soldiers fire shots at us from the plaza. I turn to the right, detouring from the route that Skye and the others are taking back to avoid the bullets. I navigate my way between a set of walkways that connect three adjacent buildings and then swerve back to the left toward where Skye is.

I glide up to them on a wide, busy street. People on the sidewalk below us shout up, pointing their fingers and taking pictures. We ignore them and continue on our route back to the embassy. I find myself worrying about where Hunter is, but I force the thought to the back of my mind.

A massive explosion rocks the city, and up ahead of us, a chain of buildings go up in flames. Glass shards hurl in every direction, and the smell of smoke burns my nose. I angle myself fully downwards towards the street. I raise my arms, flattening the chute so that I slow down. I reach the ground in a matter of seconds, and when my feet hit the sidewalk, I turn my eyes to the complex in front of me.

The entire American embassy is alight with fire, its buildings completely destroyed. The entirety of the west wing is now only a skeleton of what it once was, and the east side is crumbling as well. Men and women are being evacuated out of the embassy, police and soldiers alike ushering them into ambulances. Screams echo across the streets, along with the whir of sirens.

My eyes turn upwards to the sky, where I can see two fighter jets circling away from the city. I grimace, knowing that Laurings must have sent them as soon as I fired my shot at him. He's smart enough to know that we came from the embassy, and as a show of his strength, he put the entire city on notice of his presence.

Skye and the other two agents touch the ground next to me, shocked expressions on their faces. Skye lets out a gasp, covering her mouth with her hand.

"Laurings sent those jets, didn't he?"

I nod. "He must have an air base just outside of Tokyo, where they came from."

I pause, trying not to collapse to my knees. All around me, the cries of the wounded almost tear me apart. Skye and I both know that we're the ones to blame for the bombing.

"I was able to take out the arms dealer, at least," I say to Skye. She lifts her head. "He controlled the codes to arm the warheads they had. Laurings won't be getting another supply of missiles until he finds another arms company."

"Where do we go from here, then?" she asks me. "The embassy is completely destroyed, and we can only hope that some of them survived."

As she says this, a group of black cars pulls up to the curb. A group of soldiers emerges, their guns raised. The lead officer, a woman in a dark blue coat, nods at the soldiers, and they rush forward with cuffs.

They're here to arrest us. They likely just got reports from the embassy on the truth, and because we were on the mission, we're labeled as criminals now.

The bombing of the embassy and the destruction of part of Tokyo only make the situation worse for us. I frown. Our mission was indeed sanctioned by the embassy. The government must just be too outraged over the bombing. It would take a miracle for our commanders to get us pardoned for what's happened, even if none of it was intentional.

We're taken to a facility on the north side of Tokyo. The four of us are transported together in a military convoy, with three soldiers assigned to each of us, all armed with electrifying batons and guns. As we exit the van we're in, the same head officer who arrested us leads us inside a cluster of buildings.

As we enter the main building of the facility, each of us is taken to different wings. My guards take me into a holding area, where my arms are chained behind me and my legs strapped to a chair.

Several hours pass. I study the room around me: blank gray walls with windows, likely one-way glass. My guess is that there are still guards stationed outside of the room on a rotation every hour. I stretch my neck, my hands sore from the metal chains that are tying them together. There's a pin hidden in my hair that I stuck there just before we were arrested. Even though I could get to it, what would be the point? I have no way out of this room, and any more conflict would just be worse for the NAIS to deal with.

I let out a long breath when the door to the room finally opens. A very familiar woman steps inside, and I narrow my eyes, wondering if I'm hallucinating. The guards did inject some serum in my body before I got put in here, likely to make me more compliant to questioning. After I blink several times, I realize that the woman is indeed who I think it is, my lead commander. Evelyn Taylor. She must have come all the way from our base in Australia.

"What a mess you've gotten us into August," she says with a deep sigh.

A guard follows her inside and walks over to me. They untie me from the chair, and I stand up, rubbing my wrists.

Taylor continues. "The Japanese government is currently filing a report for a D16," Taylor says. "A D16 represents that a foreign intelligence agency has caused an act of terrorism on Japanese soil. Our government is shutting down all NAIS operations because you and the people at the American embassy didn't ask permission before going through on your mission." She comes closer to me, looking straight into my eyes. "Do you have anything to say for yourself, August?"

I straighten my stance, confused. "The mission was sanctioned. That's what the people at the embassy told us," I say to her.

While Taylor is my commanding officer, she doesn't scare me at all. If there's something strange going on, I'm going to figure it out.

"My agents stopped an arms deal between Laurings and another group."

She stares at me incredulously. "Do you not get what I'm saying? The NAIS is being suspended for foreign crimes, and you are being taken back to the States to be tried for treason against the Japanese government. You and your associates will likely be sent to prison for four months before being released. And in addition to this, you'll be banned from ever setting foot on Japanese soil again."

The weight of this punishment hits me hard. It might not even be fair. The others and I will be tried in court for supposed treason and considered criminals. Criminals.

Never before in my life have I been accused of something against the law, and now I know that I should have called Taylor before the mission to get it sanctioned. I cringe inwardly at my mistake, wondering whether there's any way I can fix the situation. It's jarring how quickly things can change.

EIGHT

Several hours after Taylor came to my holding room, I'm escorted out of the facility and onto another convoy of black cars. From there is a half-hour drive through the surrounding mountains to a long airfield where a long military plane is waiting on the tarmac. The guards shove me out of the car I'm in, keeping their hands on my shoulders as I'm taken up the plane's boarding ramp. Skye is brought out of another car, and she gives me a grim nod.

Once we're aboard the plane, we're taken to the front section, three rooms behind the cockpit. Another holding cell is waiting for us here, a fairly wide room with one small window looking out at the plane's exterior. The guards leave us in here, our hands still cuffed, then shut the door and lock it.

"This isn't right," Skye says, shaking her head. "They know that our mission was for the benefit of the entire world. They know Laurings is a terrorist."

I swallow, feeling a wave of guilt wash over me. I brought her into this, and it's not fair that she should be imprisoned just like me.

"Skye, I'm sorry that I asked you to come back to the agency. "

She looks me in the eyes. "It's not your fault, August. You didn't know that the consequences would be so harsh."

I'm silent as the plane starts down the runway. Why is it that we get to bear the consequences of Laurings' actions? The NAIS isn't doing the right thing here. We didn't commit treason; we did exactly as the embassy wanted us to do.

I glance outside the window, studying the black vehicles that make up the military convoy that had brought us here. On each of their hoods isn't the Japanese military symbol; it's something else. And then I think about this plane, what model it is. My brain starts to go into overdrive, thinking about all of these details. This plane can't carry enough fuel to get us back to the States.

"We're being framed," I say.

Skye looks up at me, a questioning look on her face.

"Taylor, the convoy, this plane," I continue. "We're not going back to America; we're being taken somewhere else."

Skye frowns at me. "What do you mean by that?"

"Think about it. The cars outside, they're not Japanese military. This plane isn't designed to bring us all the way back to somewhere in the States. And Taylor was the only NAIS operative they sent here to retrieve us? These people aren't working for our agency; they're working for someone else." I pause, thinking through what I'm saying. "Our mission was sanctioned, and these people that Taylor is working with want us out of the picture. We didn't commit anything illegal; it's just that the mission didn't go as planned."

The look on Skye's face is in agreement. "You're right. The mission did get sanctioned by the embassy."

I nod at her. "We need to find a way off of this plane before we get to wherever they're taking us to."

Now, I take my cuffed hands and pull the pin from my hair, and Skye grins at the sight of the metal lock pick. I insert the pin into the lock on my cuffs, and they clink, loosening. I pull off the cuffs and then unlock Skye's too.

"What can we do now?" she asks me, keeping her voice down.

I glance around the space we're in, searching for anything of use. My eyes go to the pipes lining the top of the room, likely ventilation for the rest of the plane. Skye follows my gaze to them as well, and now we both know that we can get out of here.

"Alright," I say, taking the pin and standing up. "Once I puncture those pipes, the ventilation on the plane will destabilize, and they'll send people to check it out. When they come through, we'll take care of them and take their weapons. From there, we'll have to make it to the cargo bay, where we can parachute out. But to get there, we'll have to get past at least five armed guards. Should be doable, right?"

Skye lets out a short laugh and then nods. "Sounds like a plan."

I take the pin and push it hard into a weak point in the piping structure. Clear gas floods out of the shafts, and a small alarm goes up outside. I hear shouts, then the rush of footsteps. I hold up a hand at Skye, signaling for her to be ready.

The door to the room flies open to reveal two guards. I rush for the one on the left, tackling him into the wall. I kick the door shut, then send my fist right at his jaw. The man buckles, and I finish through with a knee to his stomach.

Next to me, Skye's guard is also lying on the floor of the plane, unconscious. I kneel down, taking the man's firearm. I nod at Skye, then pull open the door and step into the hallway.

The space is clear for now, but the sound of more alarms has gone up. We both run down the left side towards the cargo bay. When a guard steps into the hallway from a separate room, I don't hesitate before sending a bullet into his stomach. He falls aside, and Skye and I push past.

Two more guards emerge into the hallway ahead of us, their guns up. We both duck into a room on the right for cover as bullets fly past us. The guards come around the corner, and as they do, we gun them down immediately.

Several more soldiers interrupt our route to the cargo bay, which we easily take care of. After around a minute of running, we finally reach the cargo bay. We come into the large space, our weapons up. A singular guard occupies the space, and Skye shoots him before he can raise his weapon.

My eyes go straight to the center of the cargo bay, where a massive jeep-like vehicle is positioned atop a wide metal pallet. The car is hooked down onto the pallet, and on each corner of it lies a parachute cable. It's a military vehicle that Skye and I are both familiar with.

"Let's take this," I say to Skye, pulling open the front seat door. She climbs in next to me, and I turn on the ignition. As the jeep's engine is starting, I head to the control console on the right wall, then open the cargo bay.

The wide ramp at the front of the cargo hold opens downwards, revealing the clouds and wind outside. I climb back into the jeep and put it in reverse. As I'm doing this, shouts come from in front of us, and a group of guards emerges from the central hallway of the plane, their weapons up. Bullets spray toward us, but I don't flinch. The windshield holds steady, and the bulletproof glass shields us from the oncoming fire.

I push down on the accelerator, and the jeep begins to roll backward down the ramp. I search for a particular knob on the console next to me, and when I find it, I pull hard down on it.

The top of the jeep opens up above my head, and a turret emerges from the roof. The small cannon whirs outside and then fires a single missile into the cargo bay of the plane. The entire back of the plane erupts with flames, and just as the entire vehicle explodes from the impact, the jeep flies off of the boarding ramp and into the open air.

Skye pulls on a red handle protruding from the roof, and the jeep's parachute deploys. I hear gears turning under my seat as a black chute emerges from the bottom side of the jeep. The massive cloth sheet catches the wind, and our descent slows.

I take a look outside the windows. We're in a dry, mountainous area that I would guess is somewhere in Asia, given that we've just come from Tokyo. The wind outside roars, and it'll be at least several more minutes before we reach the ground.

"Where to now?" Skye asks me. She's noticed that I've been studying our surroundings. "Do we have any contacts in this area?"

I frown, trying to get the location tracking on the jeep's console to work. As it comes online, I can see that we're near the western part of Myanmar, right below where the Himalayas mountain range runs across the continent of Asia. Thoughts run through my head, and I remember that any NAIS contacts are out of the question. We're most likely fugitives now, and Taylor probably has a search group out to look for us.

"There is a man named Tristan," I say to Skye. "He's an old friend that'll welcome us. I think he can get us equipment and information that we need."

I look outside of the window again. Another minute and we'll be on the ground.

"According to this jeep's GPS, we'll have to drive sixty miles south to reach the coast. From there, we can find Tristan in a seaside town called Tyrus."

Skye nods at me. "Alright, let's get to it then."

After we reach the ground, I step outside to disassemble the parachute, which I store in the jeep's trunk. From there, we take a long, rocky path toward the coast. Fortunately, the vehicle is designed for off-road terrain, and its large wheels have no problem getting us across the desert area at sixty miles an hour.

Two hours pass by the time we drive into Tyrus. It's a modestly-sized outpost along the coast of the ocean, but its roads and buildings are running with advanced modern technology. As I remember from my last visit to Tristan, this town is actually known for being home to many good sources of information.

As I look around the city, I'm relieved that there doesn't seem to be any military presence here. We won't have to worry about being stopped as we head to Tristan's house. People on the street nod at us and wave as they continue doing their business. I continue down the path through the town until we reach the east side.

Tristan lives in a large, modern estate on the very corner of the town, right where the ocean meets a broad hill. The outskirts of his home are surrounded by a short brown fence, more for show than security. Two guards stand in front of the mansion itself. One of them waves us into a parking space, clearly unnerved by the large military jeep we're in.

We get out of the car as they walk up to us. The one in front waves a small round device in front of each of us, checking us for weapons. I guessed they'd do this, so to avoid any complication, Skye and I left our firearms in the back of the jeep.

The doors to the estate swing open, and a tall man with wide shoulders walks out, another bodyguard at his side. His hair is long and wavy like mine, though he's noticeably older, with a short, neatly trimmed beard. Tristan's blue eyes always seem so sharp and alert, but when he sees me, he claps his hands.

"August," he says, stepping forward and giving me a short embrace. "I hear you're being hunted by your own agency, yes?"

I nod at him, my lips curved grimly. "Skye and I came to you because we need intel and equipment. And because Taylor and the rest of her agency are working against us, I figured you'd be willing to lend some help. Especially after I saved your life in Austria."

Tristan grins. "Ah, August, just as I remember. Always using the past as a tool." He pauses. "Though you did save my life, and for that, I'm grateful."

Tristan gestures for us to follow him into the house.

The inside of the mansion is wide and polished. We emerge into a large living room decorated lavishly with paintings and glass sculptures. A long glass stairway leads down from the floor above, and from under it rushes water, acting as an indoor waterfall. Tristan comes from an extremely wealthy family. He works for the United Nations, though he's still allowed to dabble in private conflicts such as the one we're going through now.

Tristan takes us up the stairs and onto a balcony, where he motions for us to sit on a set of long couches. I sit on a couch to the left, and Skye settles in beside me. I tap my earbud, hoping no one notices. Tristan rests comfortably in an armchair across from us.

His eyes wander across the balcony to the setting sun. I glance out at the beautiful horizon, where the waves lap against the shore with the sun's last rays reflecting across the water.

"Beautiful, isn't it?" Tristan says.

"It is," Skye replies.

Tristan crosses his legs, his gaze now setting on us. "But the sunset isn't what you two are here for. You two, despite being international criminals, want me to tell you where Oscar Laurings is."

And just as I remember Tristan. Always seeing straight through the people around him, like our minds are transparent and open to him. This is why he works for the UN because he can understand what others are thinking so well. This is why every time I need information, I come straight to him because I know he'll have it.

I sigh. "Well, because you know what we want, does that mean you're willing to help us in finding what information we need?"

"See, August, what you're asking isn't all that simple. Laurings isn't a man that's easy to find, and besides, what's in this for me? The delight of aiding wanted fugitives and getting arrested for it?"

He does bring up a good point. Just because I saved his life doesn't mean that his information comes free. He could report us right now to his higher-ups at the UN, and we wouldn't be able to do anything. The entire estate is heavily guarded, and Skye and I couldn't make it five steps before we had security on us.

Coming to Tristan was a gamble, but I'm always prepared. Like Tristan, I think three steps ahead of everyone else, devising the most efficient plans with the least amount of collateral damage.

"Because, since the beginning of our conversation, I've been recording your every word. The channel that my recording is on runs straight through to our military jeep, and if you do so much as touch me, I'll send the audio straight to the United Nations headquarters in Boston." I smile, and Tristan frowns.

"I have to admit, August," he says. "Very well thought out."

Skye nods at me. "And," she adds. "We would feel bad for blackmailing you into helping us. When we catch Laurings, we'll tell your UN superiors that you were the one who supported us."

Tristan crosses his arms. "Well, you two aren't giving me much choice, right?" He pauses, contemplating what we're asking him to do. "I can get you Laurings' location, but I want payment. Two million."

"Done," I say. The money is well worth it. "We'll get you the money as soon as we get his location, and we're on our way. I'll transfer you half now as proof."

"So we have a deal, then," Tristan says to us. "Follow me."

We stand up as he leads us off of the balcony. The guards accompany us into an elevator that heads downward into the underground of the house. The doors slide open, and I step out into a wide cavernous area. In the center of the space is a large desk with four computer monitors mounted on top of it. Each screen displays glowing blue text that is shifting every second. The middle of the desk is occupied by a small laptop, which looks small in comparison to the other computers.

Tristan pulls an office chair in front of the desk, and Skye and I move to either side of him, our eyes on the monitors in front of us. Tristan types in code to the laptop, and as he does, the screen to the far right changes, its blue text replaced by a long bio. I recognize the face on the screen as Laurings instantly, and information about him shows next to the image. He's wanted for three dozen known murders, illegal shipments of weapons, and bombing. At the moment, he's third on Interpol's wanted list.

I look away, knowing that Skye and I make up the first two spots. I never imagined being a wanted criminal after all of the years I trained for the NAIS. Skye is silent for a moment as well, and I promise myself that whatever it takes, I'll at least get her name pardoned.

I turn my attention to the other screens. Tristan is still typing commands into the system, and he pulls on a pair of glasses, seemingly in deep concentration. Security footage is pulled up on a screen to the left, and Skye and I shift our focus to it. I see a wide street bustling with people and a long body of water running next to it. A pier stretches out into a harbor, and behind it, I can see the outline of a long bridge with cars running along it. I turn my gaze to the sky, which is a shade of gray with clouds.

"Where is this?" I ask Tristan.

"San Pablo, Argentina. Watch the pier," he says. "This footage is from half an hour ago, and the system gave me facial recognition on the man getting into this boat."

Tristan points to a tall man wearing a long jacket, his head covered in a hood. The camera zooms in as Tristan types something into his keyboard. Then the image of the man's face is enlarged as well, and sure enough, I can see the resemblance. Tristan puts in another command, and a face recognition program comes up. It's an eighty percent match.

"This is the only footage of Laurings that I can find from the past three days," Tristan tells us, pausing the scene. "He must've only been in the camera's view because he needed to be at this dock."

Tristan continues playing the footage. I watch as Laurings steps into a black boat piloted by another hooded man. The motorboat glides through the harbor to a connecting canal that runs alongside a boardwalk.

"There's no cameras along the harbor that have a view of him?" I ask Tristan.

He shakes his head at me. "No, unfortunately not. Though I did find another piece of short footage that came from five minutes ago. We can likely confirm that Laurings is in San Pablo. See, the man is wearing the same outfit and is still matching."

He types in a command, and this time, the screen directly in front of me displays the video.

Laurings steps out of the motorboat, and I catch the silver gleam of a pistol in his back pocket. The hooded figure from the boat accompanies him as they step onto the boardwalk. The camera then loses sight of them once more.

"Are you monitoring the boardwalk?" Skye leans forward, studying the scene. "Any matches since then?"

Tristan shakes his head.

I clap Tristan on the back. "Thanks for your help." I glance at Skye. "Can you get us a plane to San Pablo?" I ask.

"I knew you were going to say that." Tristan sighs. "I can get you a ride there. Oh, and there's one more thing you should know."

"What's that?"

"Your friend, Hunter. He's alive, and Laurings has him."

I narrow my eyes. "And how exactly do you know that?"

Tristan meets my gaze, his lips pressed tightly together. "I have my sources."

NINE

We touch down in San Pablo at a private airport a day after visiting Tristan. We're driven to the central section of the city by Tristan's soldiers, nearing the harbor that we'd seen Tristan's footage of.

I recognize the harbor immediately. It's a wide port area with dozens of piers and boats floating in the gentle water beside the marina. People mill around, doing their general work. I can make out the bridge from the scene. But nothing out of the ordinary—not even a conspicuous black motorboat or an internationally-wanted killer. Imagine that.

"Come on," I say to Skye. "Let's head to the boardwalk."

I keep the route that Laurings took in my head, remembering that he boarded the motorboat onto a canal that paralleled the boardwalk. We pass by colorful buildings and expansive gardens on our way there. Children and adults play out on the smooth sand of a beach, and surfers wade out into the ocean to catch waves.

The wooden planks underneath my feet creak as we step out onto the boardwalk. Shops, restaurants, and some plain commercial buildings line the left side of the walkway, a metal railing overlooking the ocean on the right.

It takes me several moments to catch the scent of gunpowder in the air. Skye seems to notice it too, and I crouch to the floor, searching for where the smell is originating from.

"Did you find something?" Skye says.

I narrow my eyes as I peer through the cracks between the wooden planks of the walkway. I lay my hands on the planks, trying to find an opening between them.

She kneels down next to me as I study the planks. People around us just steer away from us, giving us strange looks. I guess it isn't every day that you see folks at the beach studying the floor.

Finally, I find a loose plank. I gesture to Skye, and she shuffles over. I put my fingers underneath the walkway and pull up on the plank. It lifts to reveal a ladder that descends into darkness.

I stare into the murky tunnel. Skye nods at me. She climbs in first, lowering herself inside. I go in after her, and I pull the wooden plank that I removed back in place. The scent of gunpowder is stronger down here, and my hands begin to sweat as I climb down the metal ladder.

"I'm at the bottom," Skye calls from several feet below me.

I step off the ladder gently as I reach her. Light still filters through the cracks in the boards above us and into a large underground space about fifteen feet tall. At the end of the huge room, a door leads somewhere else. I glance back up at the ladder that we came down through, and something catches my eye.

I turn back towards the ladder and my eyes land on a piece of curved metal with engravings on it. It's hanging on the side of one of the ladder rungs so that we wouldn't have felt it coming down. I pull it off and hold it in my hand. Skye walks over to me at my pausing.

"Do you know what it is?" Skye asks.

"Yeah, it's familiar." I squint, holding it up to the light. "We had some of the ops agents look into the structure of the Shadow Group a while back. Members wear these pins as a symbol of rank. And there's only one person with this one."

I point to the skull stylized in gold. A red arrow runs through the skull, and long black swaths run along the edges of the arrow.

"What rank is it?"

"This bears the rank of commander," I say.

She furrows her brow. "So now we know definitively that Laurings was here."

"Laurings must've dropped it when he was climbing down. It's safe to infer that he was here." I tuck the pin into my pocket.

Skye and I walk toward the door at the end of the room. When I turn the handle, the door doesn't move. Skye hands me a small tube-shaped device, and I attach it to the door. Three pronged arms emerge from the body of the device and latch onto the door's handle. A whirring sound echoes throughout the room and the arms slowly break apart the lock on the door. After it's finished, I turn the handle again, and the door swings open.

The room we emerge into is even larger than the first. The walls stretch at least twenty-five feet into the air. Lanterns hang at intervals along the walls. Aside from the gunpowder that I'd detected earlier, the tangy smell of blood also lingers. I notice something lying in the corner of the room. I pull my gun from its holster and approach it cautiously.

It's a body. A man lies slumped over on his back on the ground, blood gushing from a wound in his side. I beckon to Skye, then lean down next to him.

I quickly roll him over to study the wound. Bullet. I pull a piece of cloth from my belt, then wrap it around his waist and put pressure on it. He was hit recently.

"I recognize him," I tell Skye as she crouches next to me. His oily black hair and deep olive skin are easy to pick out. "He was at the arms meeting in Tokyo."

Skye gives me a puzzled look. I keep trying to put pressure on the man's wound, but too much blood is flowing out.

"But then, who shot him?" she asked.

"Laurings must've. I think that he didn't want us to use this man to track him, sort of like securing a loose end."

I put my hand on the dying man's neck, trying to find a pulse. His heartbeat is weak but still alive. I pull a syringe from my belt, then inject it into his arm. It should give him a small boost.

The man's eyes flicker open, and he takes several rapid breaths. He shakes his head at us in disbelief. Almost in a daze, he rasps, "Laurings shot me."

"We know. Can you tell us where he went?"

For a second, I feel as though he won't reply. Then he gives a slight tilt of his head.

"NAIS Base 40C," he says in between ragged breaths. "And there's one more thing."

We wait.

"Laurings is heading to these coordinates." He produces a small piece of parchment from his pocket and hands it to us. "He doesn't know that I have that," he adds, nodding tiredly at the parchment.

Then his eyes take on a gaunt look, and his breaths slow until they finally stop. I close his eyelids. Skye and I exchange a glance.

"So Laurings did kill him?" Skye says, standing up.

"Yeah. I know the base he mentioned. We need to go there. It's just two miles from here, on the west side of the city's mountain range. We should at least go before we leave for these other coordinates."

"Alright. But what happens if they don't welcome us? What do we do if we're arrested on sight?"

I shrug. "We're going to need answers either way. I don't have any idea what's going on with the world right now, but I'd guess that we'd at least be filled in if we get caught."

I give her a pointed look and begin walking back toward the ladder we came through. I pull myself up the rungs, and Skye follows me. I push up on the wooden plank that covers the tunnel and replace it as both of us emerge into the sunlight.

As I'm opening my mouth to ask Skye what method of transportation she'd like to use to reach the base, I feel the ground underneath me shake like thunder. The planks beneath my feet begin to splinter into dozens of jagged pieces of wood, the cracking of the boards roaring in my ears. Screams erupt from the beach and the buildings around me.

I grab Skye's hand, and the two of us sprint down the crumbling boardwalk, barely reaching asphalt before the entire structure collapses. My eyes sweep our surroundings. Massive trees come tumbling down in columns, the rubble from already crumbling buildings piling into a dusty haze that makes everything blurry. I'm about to run into a solid-looking complex with Skye when I hear a scream.

"What is it?"

"Get to cover," I say without explanation. "I'll be right back."

I don't give her a chance to reply before I'm running toward the sound. My ears strain as the destruction around me becomes deafening. Huddled underneath a fallen store sign is a little girl, unlikely beyond the age of ten. She covers her ears with her hands.

When she sees me, I see some type of hope in her eyes. I offer her my hand, and she takes it gladly, but I decide to hoist her onto my back instead. I rush back in the direction I came. A huge white pillar falls across the street and obstructs my path. A piece of metal shrapnel gouges itself into my ankle, and my legs buckle for a moment. I grit my teeth through the pain and remind myself of the two lives I'm trying to save.

The girl screams in terror, which certainly doesn't help, but I block out the noise and scramble with her up a flight of stairs. When we reach the top of a small bridge, I spot Skye waving to me from under the awning of a building. I spring towards her.

The shaking intensifies tenfold, and now the ground is so unstable that I can't step without tripping. I carry the girl into an alley, where we crouch together underneath an overhang. I feel the wall of the building next to me beginning to crack from the pressure, and my heart beats so fast I think it'll explode from my chest. I shut my eyes, clutching this small girl who I don't know tightly in my arms, a desperate gesture that I hope might bring her comfort. There's nothing I can do. It's in the hands of Mother Nature now.

The rumbling and shaking cease. I open my eyes to find that the rattling is gone and that the girl is still next to me, shaken but safe. I hear footsteps, and Skye rushes into the alleyway. She's alright. She helps up the girl, then me, and I step out into the street. People begin to emerge from the nearby buildings, seemingly entranced with the idea that the shaking has stopped. We're all safe now.

"August," Skye says as we leave the police department where we've dropped off the girl.

I'm still thinking about the terror in her eyes, how she clung to me like her last hope. At least tonight, I'll sleep knowing that I saved her life.

"Yeah?"

"So I was thinking," Skye says, more to herself than me. "Do you think these earthquakes have something to do with the files? It feels like it could all be connected."

"These" refers to the dozens of earthquakes that occurred across the world in the span of several hours. It's an unprecedented amount of tremors; it's the only time in human history that such a thing has happened. Definitely not a coincidence.

"I wouldn't say it's out of the question," I reply. "You still wanna pay a visit to that base?"

She nods. "Maybe we'll find answers there."

The smell of smoke is putrid in the air as Skye and I crest a hill leading up to the base.

The base that Laurings' victim had told us about lies up ahead of us, its main structure nestled up against the side of a mountain. The smoke I had caught the scent of is streaming out the side of the base's complex. Every building in the east wing is burning and alive with flames. Fire dances alongside tall white columns and snakes along the mountainside, lighting trees ablaze in a wave of an inferno. Fractured support beams and plating lie scattered around the base, and guards lay sprawled on the grass out in front, their blood pooling around them. Two towers, presumably what was part of the command section of the base, have collapsed into each other, and I watch in silence as one of them plunges into a river, dragging the other with it. A splash erupts at the bottom of the gorge beneath the base, and the crumbling pieces of stone move downriver.

But all of this destruction isn't from the shake. As we made it here, there were no signs of the earthquake along the way. It seems to have only affected the city of San Pablo itself.

I can make out the sound of shouts echoing from across the gorge. Skye rushes over to me, her eyes surveying the situation just like mine.

"Laurings must've wanted to make a statement or display firsthand the resources he has at his disposal." I point at a long metal bridge that leads across the gorge. "Come on, we need to go help them."

Skye and I run across the bridge in the direction of the base. When we finally reach the other end of the gorge, my heart is beating fast. I don't stop to breathe. There are people dying inside of this base right now.

We now emerge onto a mountainside path that connects to the base. I continue springing forward towards the voices up ahead. An NAIS soldier's body lies in front of us to the left of the path. Bullets have torn holes in his torso.

I find an entrance on the north side of the base's complex. I shove aside wiring and broken scaffolding. Sparks fly across the ground from destroyed computers and lights.

The shouts are still coming from up ahead. I keep a hand on the pistol tucked behind my back.

"Don't move," someone says.

I hear the click of guns resounding in the darkness of the base's hallways. Skye and I lift our hands into the air. There are too many of them to fight off by ourselves.

A tall man emerges into the light. His dark green eyes seem to study us as he holds a rifle in our direction. The man looks like he's in his late forties, and he has a wide beard and a trimmed haircut. He's wearing a sleek gray vest with the NAIS eagle insignia emblazoned on it. He wears the rank of commander. I notice a string of gold badges running down the side of the vest; he's decorated.

He approaches us slowly. Two soldiers emerge from either side of him, each of them also holding guns. The man narrows his eyes at us.

"I recognize you two," he says. "You were the agents that screwed up in

Tokyo." He pauses, stepping behind each of us. He takes our guns and hands them to the others. "Fortunately for you, I don't believe a word that Taylor says. You two can put your hands down now."

I lower my hands, confused. "What do you mean you don't believe what Taylor says? She's one of the lead commanders in our agency."

The man shakes his head. "I can explain my thoughts to you. Follow me to the CIC."

We follow the man as he leads us to the command center. Dead soldiers lay slouched against the walls. I point my flashlight down a hallway, where a broken holotable lies smashed into a door. A red sign that reads COMMAND lies on its side in the empty doorway. I grimace, continuing to follow. Behind the doorway, two men lie sprawled on their backs, bullet wounds dotting their chests. Their eyes lie wide open in terror. I kneel down and close their eyes gently, then continue on.

More men lie inside the command center, all dead. Shattered screens line the walls, some of them still displaying hazy footage of the base's grounds. Smoke rises from a broken server rack to the left while sparks fly from a small power generator on the ceiling.

"My name is Thaxter," the man in charge tells us. "I'm in charge of this base." He shakes both of our hands.

Thaxter gestures to a table in the center of the room. The metal edges of the table have been broken off, and the glass making up the surface of it is shattered. I sit down in one of the chairs surrounding the table.

Thaxter had mentioned that he doesn't believe anything that Taylor says. Does he have some sort of grudge against her, or does he have a specific reason for his distrust?

"Alright," Thaxter says, leaning over the table.

His eyes analyze us. Skye and I straighten in our seats.

"You two were arrested in Tokyo and brought to a facility where Taylor met you, correct?"

When both of us nod in return, he continues. "And seeing as you were arrested, I would guess that she didn't try arguing in your favor."

We don't respond to him, but I give a nod.

He pauses once, clearing his throat. "Over the past year, I've noticed that Taylor has constantly been late to meetings and that a large portion of the NAIS funds is going to a project called Rising Star. I tried to look into the project in the NAIS files, but access to it is completely restricted." "So you think that Taylor is working on something that she's keeping hidden?" I ask.

Thaxter nods. "That's exactly what I think is going on. I've known Taylor for a long time, and I can tell that she's up to something. She's not the same good agent she used to be. I asked her about the program Rising Star, and she tried to avoid the topic. I think she's dirty with something. Now, I think whatever she's doing is separate from the entire fight with Oscar Laurings."

Skye taps her fingers against her chair. "Okay. In the past week, we've been attacked by an agency completely separate from the Shadow Group. Do you think that Taylor could be affiliated with them?"

Thaxter seems to take that in. "I would certainly agree that it's a possibility. But we can't learn anything new about Taylor until the next time I see her. Once I see her in person, it'll be easier to tell if she's lying."

"Do you know if it was the Shadow Group that attacked the base?" I ask.

"It was the Shadow Group. They had helicopters and cars with their symbol displayed all over them."

Thaxter grabs a small remote and points at a screen hanging to our right. The screen flickers on and plays some video footage.

The footage starts by displaying the grounds. Everything is going as it usually does—guards patrolling the base, agents moving between buildings. After several seconds, an explosion sounds from one of the buildings, and it bursts into flames. Men scramble all around the base, shouting to one another. A massive plane emerges out of the clouds hanging overhead, flanked by a group of fighter jets. A strafe of missiles fly in the direction of the base, and a long convoy of black military vehicles comes into view. They cross the bridge as the planes lay down cover fire. Soldiers climb out of the cars in overwhelming numbers. Within minutes, guards are sprawled along the base, and buildings are crumbling to the ground.

"It happened a couple of minutes before you came, in the aftermath of the earthquake. They arrived as an organized group," Thaxter says, switching the footage off. "Their planes were completely cloaked with a technology we had no counter for. The outer posts around the base must've been taken down as well, and they disabled our radio communication too." He shakes his head. "Hundreds of men and women, dead in a matter of a minute. Laurings and his organization are stronger than we thought they were, and he put our entire agency on notice that they're prepared to fight us if we get in their way."

"But what does Laurings want?" I ask him. "What are we fighting them for? I can't just keep doing my job without knowing why I'm doing it."

Thaxter nods at me. "You two are good agents. That's why I'm trusting you. Laurings is after File 338, the twin and failsafe file to File 337. As you may remember, he attained the first file several weeks ago during a White House raid."

"What's on the files?" Skye asks him. "And don't give us the normalcy of 'that's classified.' The situation we're in right now is far from what we're all used to."

"I don't know what's on the files," Thaxter replies. "None of us do, aside from the director, Taylor, and their closest group. They keep both of them heavily guarded in two very different places. I'm not even sure where the second one is."

"So where will you go from here? We're heading to a pair of coordinates. We have reason to believe that Laurings is trying to reach them," I say.

Skye glances at me. "But it could be a trap."

I shake my head. "Laurings' man wouldn't have set us up after being shot by Laurings himself."

Thaxter returns his gaze to me. He shakes his head, looking at the soldiers around him. All of their faces are gaunt with shock, and some of them have bloody streaks running down their cheeks. This is a group that has lost everything—their base, their comrades. They must all be just as confused as Skye and I are. There's too much going on in the world right now.

"We can escort you to your coordinates," Thaxter says. "All of our operations have been suspended now that we know the agency is corrupt. Once you track down Laurings, we can stay together." He gestures at the soldiers staring at us. "There's less than a dozen of us left."

"Can we trust you?"

Thaxter pauses, leaning back in his chair. He looks into my eyes. In them, I see a man that has experienced hardship and fought back against injustice. Somehow, I feel as though I know him.

"I'll do my best to help you with what you need," Thaxter replies, keeping his voice even. "So will the men and women that are left here."

All around me, the soldiers who have survived all nod in unison. They raise their arms to their temples and salute. It's a beautiful sight to see them saluting us and their commander.

Thaxter shakes my hand again. "And besides, what other option do you really have?" He casts a grin at my frown. "Let's catch this bitch."

TEN

"How'd you get these planes?" I ask Thaxter.

We're inside a military cargo plane.

Thaxter starts to run a tracking command on his computer. He and his group are still part of the NAIS, and they have complete access to the systems, it seems.

"We searched the hangar after the base was destroyed." He says these words with a twinge of anger and sadness. "There were a couple good ones left, so we settled on this one for transport."

I watch as Thaxter types the coordinates into a database. It takes several seconds to load, and when the frames settle, the screen displays a chain of islands in the Pacific Ocean, a glowing red dot hovering over the north side of a specific island.

"Hawaii?" I ask.

Thaxter nods. "If he isn't there by now, he will be soon." Thaxter seems to ponder the location on the screen. "Laurings is moving in an organized manner, and he has everything planned out exactly as he wants it. But why would he be in Hawaii?"

I exchange a glance with Skye. "I'm not sure," I reply. "But I think we need to head there to find out what he's doing."

Thaxter shakes his head at us. "We can't go there right now. Taylor and the NAIS command have locked down the airways surrounding any of the U.S. Provinces near the Hawaiian Islands. They have entire fleets of warships guarding the waters for the next three days. There have supposedly been several attacks on important military locations. I believe that Laurings and the Shadow Group are behind the attacks."

"But if Laurings was behind the attacks, how could he get through the blockade that he caused to be put into place?" I ask.

A woman that's part of Thaxter's group approaches us, a tablet in her hand. She hands it to Thaxter and gives Skye and me a nod. Thaxter studies the tablet before he broadcasts whatever's playing on it to the screen in front of us.

The screen displays an American news channel. A satellite view of the Pacific Ocean near the Hawaiian Islands plays. The wide expanse of water in the ocean is dotted with a fleet of warships surrounding the islands. I recognize them as U.S. Military. Some of them might even be NAIS Special Forces.

But the American ships aren't the only ones in the ocean. I watch as a long line of aircraft carriers and destroyers emerge on the horizon. On the bridge of each ship, the Shadow Group symbol is present. I watch as both fleets exchange fire and deploy fighter jets.

Laurings is going to war with the NAIS and North America.

ELEVEN

It's been two days since Laurings started his war with the NAIS.

A wave of sweltering heat hits me as Skye and I make our way down the boarding ramp of one of Thaxter's jets. Three soldiers step out with us.

While the warships were busy fighting, Thaxter took us around the backside of the Hawaiian islands. Taking the longer route was the only option, given that we would've been gunned down by the warships had we gone the other way. Luckily for us, there aren't any ships on this side; all of them are being devoted to the fight against Laurings.

I have a theory that I've been keeping to myself. Why are there so many American ships here, in Hawaii? And why would Laurings be sending his entire fleet here, as well? I know that Laurings' end goal is to acquire each of the Twin Files. So it could be a logical conclusion that the set of coordinates we have are also the location of one of the files.

This is supported by a satellite shot that I saw of this island. I'm not sure if the others noticed it, but when I studied the volcanoes on this island, I realized that there was some sort of complex there. When I looked further into it on the plane, the NAIS files showed that it was a research facility. But I think that's where the file is being kept.

It's possible that Laurings doesn't know exactly where in the Hawaiian islands the file is. Maybe—just maybe—I'm one step ahead of him.

Skye and the others are here because we're trying to set up an operation to board one of Laurings' ships. Our main focus right now is to learn more about Laurings and Taylor and also to attempt to free Hunter.

We make our way up the side of a tall hill that overlooks the valley below. This city lies thousands of feet below where we are, a wide expanse of skyscrapers and busy streets. To the left of the hill are a pair of volcanoes.

"Are you alright?" Skye asks.

"Yeah, I'm fine," I reply. I gesture for her to walk with me away from the group. "I think I know why Laurings is here," I whisper.

"Okay. What's your idea?"

"When I was looking at satellite imagery of the Hawaiian islands, I saw a research facility inside one of the volcanoes."

Skye tilts her head.

"I think that they're keeping File 338 inside of it. And my guess is that Laurings is here to find it."

"But then why hasn't he gone there yet?" she asks.

"I think he doesn't know exactly where on the island it's at," I reply. "But it's only a matter of time before Laurings' satellites find the image I saw."

"So, what's your plan? We can't let Laurings get his hands on that file. If he does, he'll have complete access to the project that Taylor is working on."

The other members of our group are making their way down toward the city of Kaset. We're planning on setting up a small recon station in the city, but that might change now that I've told Skye about the research facility. I stare at the pair of volcanoes to our left. My eyes search the outside of the volcano on the left. I can't see the facility from here; it's nestled along the inside of the lava-filled dome.

I turn back to face her. "We need to get inside of the complex," I say. "We're already criminals in the eyes of the NAIS, so it doesn't matter what we do now. I think we should try to get the file before Laurings can."

Before Skye can reply, a tremor rocks across the ground. I'm thrown off my feet and fall hard on my back. My head hits a sharp rock, and my vision starts to blur. The hill shakes wildly, and I hear the crunch of boulders falling. I try to stand and look for Skye, but the pain lancing through my head makes it impossible. I feel someone pulling me up. I'm carried and set into a car, which starts to drive. The car shakes and rocks from side to side, and my shoulder is thrown into the side of the vehicle. My team must be taking us to shelter.

I feel blood trickling from the back of my neck, and I grimace. I hear voices all around me as the car continues to drive down the hill. Where are we going? Maybe we're heading towards the city to find shelter.

Someone holds my arm steady and injects a needle into it. All of my senses suddenly come more alive, and my vision focuses. Whatever they injected into me must have sent a boost of energy to my head, similar to what I used back in San Pablo. But hopefully, I'm not on the brink of death like that man was.

I turn to see whoever's sitting next to me. I'm relieved to see Skye talking into an earpiece. Her face is covered in dirt and soot, and blood trickles from a wound on her forehead. She must be calling Thaxter to inform him about the tremors.

My vision blurs in and out, and I can make out buildings around us. After what feels like an eternity, the car finally stops driving. Skye kicks open the door and helps me out, shouting to the others to get inside. She carries me into a building. As I look around the place we've entered, I see other people. Some young, some older. All of them are terrified, sheltering from the quakes that are destroying their city.

I feel Skye and another soldier carrying me up a flight of stairs, and then I'm lying down on a bed. My head throbs from where I hit it. Skye presses a wet towel to where the wound is, trying to clean it before what's next. I pass back and forth between awareness and unconsciousness. I feel another injection, in my other arm this time, and this drug eases the intense pain of the wound. I bite my lip as one of the soldiers in our group, the medic, sews stitches to close the wound. Even with the painkiller, it takes everything in me not to cry out in pain. Then drowsiness washes over me, and I shut my eyes. The world fades away.

In my sleep, I dream of volcanic eruptions and terrified families running from earthquakes. Buildings crumble, and cars crash into one another. The world is of pure chaos, everything destroyed. It's not too different from how the world really is.

When I wake, Skye and the others aren't there. I reach my hand to feel the back of my head but then decide not to. Touching the stitches won't do anything for me but make me nauseous.

I sit up as slowly as possible. I rub the sleep out of my eyes and climb out of bed. I realize that the shaking has stopped, at least momentarily. I hear Skye's voice, and I look towards a balcony. Skye and the other soldiers are out there, conversing in quiet voices.

As I step outside, they smile to see that I'm awake. Thaxter gestures to a seat on the balcony next to him.

Before I say anything, my eyes are drawn to the city. It looks just like my nightmare. My eyes scan the buildings, and I struggle to find a single one that hasn't been damaged. Even now, crumbling concrete bits from the buildings are falling into the streets. Water floods through some of the buildings, and bent pillars and arches are scattered throughout.

"Was there a flood too?"

Skye nods. "The entire city was hit with the tremors, and the ocean swelled up into a flood." She looks at the building we're in now. "This building was crushed in some places, but the wing we're in is mostly intact. The storm's over, at least for now."

"Do you think this is related to the tremors that occurred several days ago?" I say to the group.

One of the soldiers, a woman with sharp blue eyes, answers. "Almost certainly."

Skye makes eye contact with me. "I told them about the research facility in the volcano. We ran a satellite scan with the few resources that Thaxter has left. There seems to be some sort of vault inside of the complex."

I narrow my eyes, thinking. "So, are we going there now?"

"Yeah, we agreed on it as a group," Skye says. She nods at the three others, including the woman who had spoken earlier. "When you were hurt, they helped us get you to safety. We can trust them."

I nod. I look each of them in the eye, and a sense of respect passes between us. They're all risking their own lives for Skye and me, people they've just known for several days fighting for a cause that's completely new to them.

"Alright," I say. "When do we leave for the volcano?"

After discussing a plan, our group packs up gear from the building and climbs into two jeeps. I look out the window at the decimated city as we drive up the side of a hill that leads toward the volcanoes. I try not to think about how many people have lost their lives because of these tremors. I close my eyes, praying there's a way to end all of this destruction.

Thaxter informed us earlier that Laurings' ships are still engaged in their fight with the American naval fleet. However, he also said that several of Laurings' ships are heading in our direction. They've likely found some sort of signal radiating from the research facility, and the ships will arrive as soon as they break through the NAIS blockade. It's only a matter of time before Laurings finds out exactly where File 338 is, and we have to get to it before he does.

When we reach the foot of the volcanoes, I open my door and step outside. The air is hot from the molten lava of the mountains in front of us. We're currently under the south volcano, which is known as 'The Queen' in English. It surfaced from the ocean around fifteen years ago.

Skye and I lead our small group up the side of it. We follow a small path marked by golden lanterns. It winds all the way around the circular exterior of the volcano and leads up to the entrance of the facility. I glance towards the ocean. I try to make out the outlines of Laurings' ships on the horizon, but it looks as though we still have some time before they break through to this island.

I step carefully on the path, wary of the bright red streams of lava running down the side of the volcano. The black rock of the volcano is jagged and hard to walk on. Sweat runs down my back from the heat.

Once we near the top of the path, we unholster our weapons and keep our guard up. I crouch and slowly make my way forward, leading the others. As I reach the flat part of the mountain top, my eyes search for any sign of the research facility. There must be something that leads down into the volcano.

A man emerges to my left. At the sight of us, he reaches to tap his earpiece. I unsheathe my knife and send it flying straight into his neck just before he manages to do it. The guard falls to the ground, and Skye helps me hide him in a bush that lies on the path we took earlier.

As I'd guessed, we find a long ladder that leads downwards into the volcano. I spot the research facility's gray outline protruding from the curved rock walls. When I lean over the ladder, I feel an intense amount of heat. My eyes move toward the center of the volcano. At the very bottom of the hollow mountain lies a pool of lava, with different streams of molten fragments flowing into it from the curved walls of the volcano.

"Follow my lead," I say.

I turn and begin to make my way down the ladder. My arms and legs move fast, and I repeat the process of stepping down and finding the next hold over and over. When the ladder finally ends, I jump down onto a wide platform that lies about halfway down the center of the volcano. A steel walkway runs out from the left side of the platform, connecting to the main complex of the facility. Skye and the rest of our group step down onto the platform.

"Where're the guards?" Kira asks, surveying the platform. She's one of the younger soldiers from Thaxter's force. "Shouldn't there be security here?"

Skye and I exchange a glance. I look out across the walkway towards the main complex.

"They probably keep most of the security in the main complex. We need to keep moving before they realize that the guard up top is missing."

I lead our group across the walkway. I keep my gun in a defensive position, wary of the guards that are almost certainly going to be surrounding the complex. As I cross the walkway, I duck into the shadows of the building at the front. I gesture for the others to crouch beside me.

"Alright," I whisper. "We're all going to stay together as a group. Move in a diamond formation. We'll make our way to the central building of the facility, which is where the file should be held. Our goal is to be as quiet as possible, but if it comes to it, there's enough of us to give them a fight for the complex." I lock eyes with each one of them. "There's no such thing as luck. Make every move quick and calculated."

I make a gesture to begin the operation. I lead the nine of us down the left side of the complex, keeping us inside the cover of the shadows. To my left, the rock wall of the volcano's insides runs red with streams of molten lava.

Unsurprisingly, the sound of footsteps echoes towards me. The noise came from up ahead, so it isn't possible that I heard our own footfalls. I keep my gun in front of me, and as I begin to hear voices, I signal to the rest of the group.

"Move into D14 formation," I tell the group quietly. "Keep your guard up and follow my lead."

The group arranges themselves like a diamond, similar to an arrowhead formation but just mirrored in the back. I lead the group at the front. There are two soldiers behind me, three after them, two after them, and finally, Skye brings up the rear.

Footsteps close in, and I reflexively swing my arm out in a punch. I hit a guard in the face, and I feel the bridge of his nose break. He falls backward, letting out a small cry. I swing my leg up into his stomach and bring down my elbow hard into his jaw. The man collapses, his face covered in blood. I catch him, then roll his body into the shadows.

Someone may have heard his voice. I move at a quicker pace now, jogging. We reach a tall gray building labeled with a sign that reads HIGH SECURITY AREA. I'm not sure what to make of the words, but if I had to guess, the file will be here. Though it's going to be swarming with guards.

I find a door on the side of the building. One of our soldiers reaches to turn the handle, but I stop him, shaking my head once. The doors could be rigged to set off alarms if they don't open.

Skye hands me a device. It's shaped like an everyday-use label printer, with a curved handle and a small screen. I tap three buttons on the side of it and push it onto the wall. Four long prongs extend from it and latch onto the door's handle. They make a quiet whirring noise as sparks fly off of the handle. I look around for any cameras, but hopefully, the shadows will obscure the footage anyway.

A small popping noise erupts from the door, and I turn the handle. The door slides open, and I stand guard as the others move into the building. Once everybody's in, I shut the door behind me and return to my position at the front of the group.

We've emerged into a long hallway outlined by glowing gold orbs placed at intervals along the walls. The lights give off an eerie buzzing sound, and my muscles tense as we move down the hall. The hallway turns after twenty yards, and I take a quick glance into the next room before we move in.

The space in front of us is wide and expansive, with high vaulted ceilings. There are two guards on either end of the space. One of them spots me looking into the room. I raise my gun and send bullets into two of them. They both tumble backward and onto the ground. Skye shoots another, but Kira doesn't react fast enough; the other guard presses a red button on his watch before she sends a bullet into him.

A loud siren echoes through the building, and I realize that we've tipped off the facility's security system. I search the room we're in, looking for any evidence of where the file could be held. I find a tall metal door that resembles the entrance to a vault.

"Walter and Casey, guard the hallway," I say.

They nod and rush back. I try turning the handle at the front of the metal door, but it doesn't budge. I look for any type of keypad on the door, but I find no such thing.

Skye approaches me, her eyes focused on a small tablet that she holds in her hand.

"There's an energy source coming from the other side of that door," she tells me. "The file is definitely in there."

"I know, but this is twenty-four-inch thick steel. Our explosives won't get through it. There must be some way to open it, though."

My eyes return to the door, and I search for anything that looks like it could help. I find the NAIS symbol on the bottom of the door, and I feel my mind wrapping around something. The NAIS logo is different here than it normally is. I study it, and I can make out some small text that reads RESTRICTED ACCESS - LEVEL 9 AGENTS ONLY. Below the logo is a small metal pad. It's a hand scanner.

"August, aren't you Level 9?" Skye asks.

I rush forward, nodding. "I am, but they might've disabled my access to the NAIS system." I place my hand on the scanner. "It's worth a try, though."

I hear a small click from the door, followed by the sound of gears clicking. I hold my breath. We need this to work.

I sigh in relief when the door swings open. It reveals a small cave inside the wall, and floating in the center of the space is a blue chip. The file itself is suspended in the air by three metal wires. It's a small device shaped like a hard drive with the number 338 engraved on it. I reach inside to pull it out. It comes forth easily, and I hold the delicate chip in my palm.

"Taylor must've left your clearance," Skye says.

I nod. "Either she assumed that we died in the plane crash earlier, or she forgot. If it's the former, there's a possibility that we're completely off of her radar."

Kiera hands me a small metal case, and I open it. There's a velvet lining inside, and I lay the chip down and then shut the case.

The two agents I'd sent to guard the hallway rush back towards us. "There's a group of guards trying to break down the door," Walter says, panting. "If you've got the file, we need to go — now."

I pocket the case holding the file and find a back door that leads out into the middle of the complex. We rush forward into the maze of buildings, the alarm blaring all around us.

I hear the whirring sound of rotors coming from above. A string of bullets flies into the first two members of our group from a helicopter. I hold an arm out to our group, stopping them from continuing forward into the line of fire. I see the Shadow Group symbol on the chopper's hull. Laurings has found the facility, and he's coming for the file. That means he's coming for us.

"This way," I say.

I lead us along the side of the volcano until we've reached the end of the facility's complex. I hear shots flying behind us, and I turn back to find the NAIS soldiers at the base firing at the chopper. It swerves away momentarily, and I turn back around. There's a wide hole in the volcano's inside wall, and it appears that there's a hallway leading out of the volcano. It must've been built as a method of transporting equipment to the facility.

The alarm continues to blare inside the hallway, and I ignore it, running as fast as I can alongside the others. I hear the shouts of guards behind us, and I hear a grinding noise from within the hallway. Without warning, a steel wall emerges from the ground as well as the ceiling. They're trying to block us off.

I jump through the small opening in between the walls. They slam together barely a second after I land.

I look at our group. Only six of us made it through, and I'm glad to see Skye here as well. We don't have time to dwell on the soldier stuck on the other side of the wall behind us. I continue to run as I realize that more walls are closing in front of us.

The six of us manage to make it through to the end of the hallway. Light shines through into the hallway, and it appears that we've come out in front of a mountainous region. There's a wide canyon in front of us made of various rock formations.

I find a path that leads into the rock structures. I carefully make my way across the path, and I become increasingly more aware of the giant canyon that lies in front of us. I keep my back to the volcano as I edge along the path toward the larger rock structures. The structure of this region reminds me of the Grand Canyon back in Arizona.

I tap my pocket, relieved that the file is still there. After five long minutes, I lead our group into a cave. I find a long underground river filled with lava that leads further into the mountains. For now, while the NAIS guards and Laurings' soldiers are looking for us, traveling next to this molten river will be the best way to get away from Laurings and his forces.

"Casey and Kiera," I say as we walk next to the river. "I want you two to bring up the rear. Stay fifty yards back, and if there's any sign of somebody following us, contact us immediately and rejoin the group." They nod back and stay behind as we continue to make our way along the lava.

Even though we're covered by the rocks above, I keep my gun up and listen intently for any outside noise. We continue next to the molten river for half an hour, following it until it ends. The caves end and bring us into a densely clustered area of rock formations. A cliff wall hangs diagonally along either side of the path that I find, and as I walk through it, I begin to feel claustrophobic. When does this canyon end and lead to a more open area?

My body tenses as I hear the whir of rotors again. Laurings and his helicopter are near, which means that they know what direction we're heading in. I hold up my hand, motioning for the group to stop moving.

My eyes move upwards, looking at what's above us. There's a small sliver of a gap in between the two cliff faces that cover us. I can hear voices and the drum of footsteps overhead. I strain my ears as I try to hear what they're saying.

The first voice I catch is an authoritative one, clearly in command. My heartbeat speeds up as I realize that Laurings is barely twenty feet above us.

"Fan out around the valley," he says. "Our priority is to obtain the file.

Shoot to maim them. We'll flush them out into an open area. They'll be heading towards the ocean, and we need to stop them before they get there."

The others in our group look to Skye and me for instructions. Clearly, Laurings wants us alive. We're probably heavily outnumbered, given that there are only six of us left. I don't know what to do.

I tap my wrist and send a message to Casey and Kiera, telling them to rejoin us. I wait for half a minute, and they come into sight.

"Alright, listen up," I whisper. "Stay together. I'm signaling Thaxter to send a chopper in order to extract us. We need to make it to the ocean. Avoid Laurings' men as much as possible, and if you're separated from the group, head north." I look each of them in the eye. "When the time comes, run like the fastest wind you've ever felt."

TWELVE

Our group continues through the pathway we're on, with two slanted rock walls on either side of us. Every so often, voices can be heard from above, and we're forced to hide in the shadows as they pass away. I take a glance at my watch. It's midday, but it'll get dark in not too long. We managed to contact Thaxter by sending him a message on the extraction, though the connection's so bad that we're unable to tell whether he sent a reply. For all we know, we could make it to the coast and be stuck there.

After another ten minutes of walking, Thaxter's voice comes through.

It's a garbled and unclear message, but he says, "I'm sending a chopper to you now. Be there within half an hour."

Soon, the path we're taking slants upward. The walls up above close in together, barely leaving five feet of space overhead. We have to crouch and slowly shuffle through the tight space, and I become increasingly aware of how easy it would be for Laurings' soldiers to shoot us dead if they find us moving through this tunnel.

After what seems like an eternity, the pathway opens up into a set of caves. Every footstep I take echoes through the long cavern, and I realize that a stream of water is winding along the side of the space. I tell the others, and we all kneel down next to the slim river. I cup my hands and lift the liquid to my lips.

Gunshots ring out across the cave. I instinctively duck and roll, trying to keep my arm up to shield myself. Kiera jumps in front of me, shielding me with her body. She's hit by a wave of bullets, and she collapses. I roll behind a tall rock in the corner of the cavern, and I hear shouts echo around me. Laurings' soldiers have found us.

I look around for Skye and the others. I see Kiera's dead body lying in the middle of the cavern. Her face is twisted in a scream, and the ground around her is stained scarlet. I spot Skye and Casey on the other side of the cave. Both of them have their guns out, and they're returning fire.

The realization that there are only five of us left is daunting. Laurings must have dozens of soldiers. Our chances of making it to the coast are becoming slimmer. I think back to all of my previous missions, though, and that's where I remember that hope is always there.

I signal to Skye that I'm going to make a distraction by waving three fingers at her. I pull my gun from its holster and turn on its flashlight. The bright light illuminates the area around me, and I feel bullets pelting the rock I'm crouching behind. The light gave away my position, just as I'd anticipated.

Skye sees them focus in on me and leads Casey down the right side of the cavern. I hear shouts as Laurings' soldiers lose sight of them. They become confused and begin to let random strings of bullets fly into the darkness. Their guns don't have lights attached to them; it's at least one advantage that we have over them.

As Skye and Casey continue their flank, Denis and Atusha keep laying down cover fire with their rifles. I hold my pistol steady, then turn down the left side of the cave, where the shadows completely blanket everything from sight. I continue flanking from my side as Skye takes out three of the soldiers from behind their line. They turn around to fire back at her but don't realize that they've left our side open until I've shot four of them.

We're converging on them from both sides. In a heartbeat, the entire group is dead without any more casualties from our side. Kiera's death hangs heavy in my heart, and as we gather the enemy's equipment, I sit down for a moment. The entire group has a moment of silence for her, and a wave of guilt washes over me. We're going to have to leave her body here, and we all know it. But we also know that her death can't be in vain —her and the others that died escaping from the base.

I walk over to Kiera's body and carefully remove her wedding ring and a small bracelet from her body. I put them in my pocket, vowing to myself that I'll return them to her family if I survive this.

"We need to get moving," Casey says, reloading his gun.

I pull a smoke grenade from one of the dead soldiers and clip it to my belt.

I nod back at him. "There's no doubt that they heard the shots. They'll be heading in our direction, so we need to be ready for another fight. Same tactics: Draw their fire, flank them, and then converge from separate sides."

The others nod in agreement.

This time, I lead the group forward through the caves, and Skye brings up the rear of the group. Though now that we're down another person, she stays with us. I stiffen at every slight sound, even if it's just a small lizard moving along the rock formations. We need to be more alert. Getting ambushed like the first time won't work again. And even if it does, we'll lose somebody. And then we'll continue to be whittled down until we're all dead. Our only chance is to make it to the coast.

After another short stretch of walking, the caves finally end. Again, the ground level rises and opens into a massive canyon full of naturally formed bridges.

Each of them is made up of rock formations and is close to fifteen meters long, and the only cover in the area are tall columns formed from more rocks. They're the bottom halves of an old complex of lava tubes that have collapsed over the past centuries. The canyon walls extend high up into the air, where the sky is visible. Light streams inside of the valley, well illuminating the bridges.

"Wait," I whisper to the group.

The five of us move into the shadows of the last cave before the valley of bridges. I point towards the side of the valley, where a group of thirteen soldiers is moving along the bridges. They each are carrying a pistol in their holsters, but their guns aren't what concern me. They're all holding a long metal weapon in their hands. I recognize them as flamethrowers. Laurings' plan was to force us out in the open using the flames.

"Good thing we made it out of the caves," Skye says, staying in the shadows. "What do we do now? Those soldiers are the last thing keeping us from the ocean."

She now raises her finger to point toward the end of the valley. An opening in the side of the valley reveals that the natural bridges lead to an exit from this rocky canyon area. I can see white sand dunes, along with gentle waves lapping against the shore. That's where Thaxter is waiting for us.

"Alright." The others group up around me.

I keep an eye on the group of soldiers. They're slowly moving along the bridges, meticulously picking their way through them so that they're safe from falling into the bottom of the valley. They seem to be nonchalant about being on guard; it's like they believe that there's no danger that we pose to them.

"Here's the plan." I keep my voice to a whisper. "Those soldiers have their guard down. As they get within range of our weapons, we're going to open fire on them. We should be able to half their numbers before they react. After they're covered by the rock pillars, I'll fire a flare to the north to distract them. But rather than open fire again, we're going to use the time to begin moving along the bridges. Use the columns as your cover, and move as fast as you can. It'll take them time to set down their flamethrowers in exchange for guns. As we make a break for the coast, we'll continue planting distractions to confuse them. If Laurings' chopper opens fire on us, then just keep moving. It's our only shot at making it to Thaxter." I look each of them in the eyes, my gaze lingering on Skye. "Run with the mentality that you're going to make it, and you will."

They all nod back at me solemnly. To be frank, I feel exhausted on the inside. Sweat runs down my back, and the events of today have drained my energy. But if I just concentrate on hope and if I'm confident in my ability to make this final step, everything will work out as I've planned.

I nod back at them. I unholster my gun and make sure it's reloaded. The others do the same. Each of them looks expectantly at me, waiting for my signal.

"On three," I tell them, raising my gun.

We all spread out in the shadows of the cave, making sure we each have a good angle to fire on the soldiers. I keep my gun steady, taking aim. I can feel my heart beating faster and faster. This is it. Our only chance at living another day.

"One," I say slowly.

I watch carefully as the soldiers cross one bridge and then start moving across another.

"Two," I say as they move behind the cover of one of the rock pillars.

My eyes narrow. As they come out from behind the column and into the open, I give the command to open fire.

"Three."

My finger goes to the trigger, and I pull it without hesitation. A string of bullets fires from our position, and I watch with satisfaction as mine hits true. Five of the soldiers go down within seconds, their bodies falling to the ground. As the rest of them move behind the pillars, I pull a flare from my belt.

I strike the flare against the wall of the cave, and it ignites, red sparks flying from it. I throw the lit flare as hard as I can into the valley, and it soars through the air, bringing with it a trail of orange light. The soldiers on the bridge shout to each other, momentarily distracted by the flare. They're scrambling to find where it came from.

"Come on." I lead our group out of the cave and into the open, where I lead us onto a bridge that hooks to the right.

The soldiers are still looking out at the flare, which has now struck the wall of the valley and is falling downwards. They scan the valley for any sign of movement, and after a short while, their eyes land on us.

Unfortunately for them, we've already made it across three bridges, almost halfway across the valley. My legs move faster than I think they have ever before, and as bullets rush towards us, I duck behind a rock structure that juts up through the bridge. The others do the same, staying close to each other while being covered by the pillar. Bits of rock and stone fly across through the air as the soldiers' bullets hit the column I'm behind.

As they stop to reload, our group begins to move again. I rush down the end of the third bridge and begin moving up the fourth one. We pause behind another rock pillar as the enemy fire initiates once more. I cover my ears at the sound of so many firing guns, and I begin to feel as though this plan could work. We just need to repeat the process of waiting until they reload, then moving forward towards the coast.

The sound of rotors spinning overhead breaks my enthusiasm. My eyes turn skyward as I see the blacked-out Shadow Group helicopter coming into sight. To my dismay, the gunmetal-colored shape of a mini-gun protrudes from the side of it. There's only one thing we can do now: Run.

Heavy bullets fly from the helicopter as it comes closer. I grab Skye's hand. We run across the next bridge. Chunks of rock break off from the bridge and fly down into the abyss of the valley. I hold a hand behind my head in vain.

Several steps ahead of me, one of our soldiers lets out a scream as a bullet pierces his chest. Blood splatters onto the ground and stains my black jumpsuit red. I don't have time to stop, and I sidestep around his falling body as it hits the bridge's rocky surface.

I pull a second flare from my belt and slam it into a rock column. It lights easily, and I throw the flaming flare upwards, sending sparks in all directions. It creates a red smoke that clouds the area above us. The fire from the chopper strays around the area that we're in, but most of the bullets don't come close to us. I've created some temporary cover.

Once the four of us emerge from the smoke, I realize that there's only a single bridge left. The bullet fire resumes from both sides, from the soldiers as well as the mini-gun. I fire back at the chopper with my own gun, and the bullets pierce its hull, making the fire from there stop for a short time.

My legs pump forward even faster as I realize that the last bridge is in front of us. At the end of it lies a large hole in the valley's wall that leads out onto the beach.

I pull the smoke grenade I'd taken from one of the soldiers earlier from my belt. It's the last thing I have to shield us from the rush of bullets. I pull the clip on it and throw it down several meters in front of me. The hazy gray smoke lasts several seconds before evaporating. One of the soldiers must've hit it by accident.

I breathe a sigh of relief. The soldiers have stopped to reload, and the chopper still hasn't resumed fire. I think we're in the clear.

And then a flash of something silver catches my eye. I watch as a figure dressed in a black suit jumps from the top of the valley's wall. I recognize him instantly as the man who's attacked Skye and me on multiple occasions now. Seeing that the soldiers aren't firing at him, I now know that he's working with Laurings.

He deploys his suit's built-in glider and soars toward us. He's moving fast, but we've almost made it out of the valley. He won't make it to us before we're out on the beach, where hopefully Thaxter is waiting.

Skye's scream rips across the canyon from behind me. I turn back. Blood rushes from her leg, and she stumbles onto the ground. We're two-thirds of the way across the bridge by now, and I pull her behind the cover of two rock formations. Bullets fly around us, hitting the rocks and sending up hundreds of pieces of debris.

Skye pushes me away. "August," she says in a rasping voice. She's clearly in a lot of pain. "You need to leave me. You can find me again." She pauses, looking me in the eyes. "I know you will."

Skye lets go of my hand, and I give her a long look. I shake my head at her, tears flooding down my cheeks. I know that I have to leave her. She'll be captured, but I have to go.

I stand up and turn towards the coast. Casey and Atusha have already made it there. Denis is running along the end of the bridge, waving for me to run forward. I do.

I cover my head with my arms as I feel a bullet skim my elbow. I'm lucky that the soldiers are so far away from me right now; their weapons aren't very accurate at this range. But even so, I keep sprinting. When I finally reach the hole in the valley's wall, I crouch behind a rock for a moment with the others to catch my breath.

I stare back towards the valley of bridges, over fifty yards away now. I see Skye lying on the ground, and it feels like a knife stabbing straight through my heart. The man in the black armor glides down towards her, landing on the bridge. He holds a gun at her face and asks her something. When she doesn't reply, he kicks her in the stomach. She cries out in pain.

Rage fills my body. I lift my gun and fire an entire magazine of bullets at the man. Two of them slam into his helmet, and I heave a breath as his mask blows off.

The armored man is Hunter.

THIRTEEN

My hands shake. The gun I'm holding drops to the ground. All I can do is stare out at the valley I just escaped from.

I look for any type of emotion on Hunter's face, but all I see is a stone-cold grimace. Nothing but a vacuous stare.

I feel hands pulling me with them, and my legs barely support my weight as I'm dragged forward toward the hole. My vision blurs. I realize that I've been shot in the stomach by one of the soldiers. I stumble, but Casey keeps me steady. I manage to walk into the valley. Pain lances through my entire body.

I hear a loud explosion behind me. I turn around to see the hole in the valley's wall collapsing. The others must have placed explosives there to seal the entrance. Now only Laurings' chopper can follow us. Good thinking.

I barely make it ten feet through the first sand dune before I collapse to the ground. I hear shouts around me, and I'm lifted onto a stretcher. I feel myself being carried off the ground, and even though my vision is blurry, I can make out the outline of a helicopter's cargo bay. Two people crouch in front of   me, and I hear the chopper's rotors begin spinning. I've made it to Thaxter.

When I wake from my restless sleep, I'm lying in bed. I try sitting up, but someone next to me holds my shoulders down. My entire body aches, and I can still feel pain coming from my stomach. I look around, my vision coming into focus.

I see Thaxter sitting on the bed next to me. He's the only other person in the room, so he must've been the one who kept me from sitting up. That's probably for good reason, though. I can't feel any of my muscles right now.

I make eye contact with him. He seems to be unharmed. My gaze drifts away. I can't look at him right now. I was leading the mission, and I managed to get the majority of our group killed.

"What happened after I blacked out?"

Thaxter stays quiet for a while before he answers. "You and three of my group made it out alive. The loss is catastrophic. As far as I know now, Laurings' soldiers have captured Skye."

He pauses again. He reaches into his pocket and pulls out a small metal case. Thaxter smiles a little bit, handing me the case. It opens easily, and inside lies the file.

All I can think about right now is the fact that Skye's sitting in some prison cell being monitored by Laurings. I brought her into this. I should be the one sitting in a blank white room right now, and she should be right where I am.

"I know that look."

My eyes return to Thaxter. "What do you mean?"

Thaxter scoots closer to me. Another small smile spreads on his face. "You love Skye, don't you?" he says.

The question surprises me. My cheeks flush red, and I move away from him. But in my heart, the question sticks with me. Do I love her?

When I don't reply, Thaxter's smile turns into a wide grin. I give him an incredulous look, and he holds his head up. I look away from him, trying to think.

I contemplate his question for a good long while. I know Skye means a lot to me as a friend, but as somebody I love in a different way? For the last two weeks that we've been together, I've hidden those feelings from her, but deep down, I didn't want to. Skye is smart and witty and beautiful. I really do love her.

I nod at him. "I guess I do."

Now a sad look crosses Thaxter's face. Maybe one of his memories has been sparked by our conversation.

"My wife was an agent too, August," Thaxter tells me. "Technically, we weren't supposed to be together. She'd gotten captured as well, not in a situation too different from Skye's. The difference was that I didn't have the courage to cross my commander's orders to rescue her. She died in the enemy's compound from a disease." He looks at me again. His gaze seems to sear into me. "You, August, have all of the courage in the world. And you are going to save Skye."

This story about Thaxter's past makes me feel sad for him. My present is bringing back his past. And what makes it worse is that his wife died.

He's right. I won't let that happen to Skye.

"Thank you," I say. "You have no idea what this means to me."

Thaxter nods. "It's good that you know how you feel about her. Is there anything else I can help you with right now? If you're fine, I'll leave you to rest."

I move my head up on my pillow a little bit. The movement makes my sore neck hurt even more. Then I remember that I'd been meaning to tell him about Hunter.

"Thaxter, Skye being captured isn't the only major thing I have on my mind. Laurings has a double agent. There's this armored soldier that keeps attacking Skye and me. But today, I saw who was under the helmet," I say.

He raises an eyebrow. "Did you recognize him?"

"It was my friend, Hunter."

At that, Thaxter frowns. "The friend you were trying to rescue back in Antarctica?" I nod. "Are you sure?"

"I've known him for a long time. But I think that Laurings has found a way to turn him to his side."

I close my eyes, deep in thought. Now all of this adds up.

"When that armored figure attacked me for the second time in Tokyo, Hunter was bruised the next day. On the mission to stop Laurings' arms dealing, it's possible that he cut his own chute so that he could stay with Laurings. What did Laurings do to him?"

Thaxter stands up and paces around the room. His forehead crinkles, further reminding me of how old he is. Even so, he feels like a mentor to me right now. I can't express in words how good it feels to have a veteran watching over me, especially in the situation I'm in. Thaxter experienced many of the things I'm experiencing now in his own past. He helped me understand my feelings for Skye, and I think he'll have something important to tell me again right now.

"There's something strange going on," Thaxter says.

At that, I give him my own puzzled look. But I think he's talking about Hunter and not the tremors and floods occurring around the world.

"How long have you known Hunter?" he asks me. "It's possible that Laurings put him into the NAIS to rat out information back to the Shadow Group."

I shake my head. "That's not possible. I've known Hunter since he was five."

"Then there are dozens of possibilities," Thaxter replies. "I think that we'll be able to discover the truth through more research. I can have my people look into Hunter's NAIS file. I'll tell you if they find anything of interest. For now, you need to rest."

I nod back at him and give my thanks for his advice. He leaves the room and turns out the lights. There are a million different thoughts running through my mind right now, and at the top of them isn't Hunter. It's Skye.

What Thaxter had said about his wife unnerves me. She died because he hadn't gone to save her. That's not what I'm going to do. I'm going to find where she's being held and bring her back.

And the hard part of that? The hard part will be telling her about how I feel.

FOURTEEN

Gunshots ring out across the airship's deck as a line of Thaxter's soldiers hold out shields to cover me from fire. I rush forward and down a flight of stairs to the lower deck, my legs carrying me as fast as possible. I need to find Skye. Quickly. Or this will all fail.

Thaxter and his group will hold off Laurings' forces while I find her. Supposedly, she's being kept somewhere in the lower levels of the ship, near where the detention block is located.

I find my way down another winding stairway, closing in on the prison sector. As I round a corner, a foot slams into my chest, and I collapse back against the wall. All of the wind is knocked out of my chest, and I rise into a defensive position.

I look up to see Skye's beautiful eyes staring back down at me. I know the look on my face must be incredulous at the moment.

"You came," she says. "Are you alright?"

I hug her tightly. "Yeah, I'm fine. Everything's happening so quickly, though. How'd you escape?"

She smiles. "While they were interrogating me, I knocked out five of them. I'm kind of impressed with it myself."

"That is impressive," I reply.

My eyes sweep the hallway around us. I see a security camera watching us. We need to go.

"We can catch up later," I add. "Follow me. We need to make it to the engine room. We're going to blow this ship. Thaxter and the others are waiting up on the deck, and we'll find them afterward. They're fighting off Laurings' soldiers, so we have to hurry."

"Blow the ship?" Skye asks. "Do you have something we can use?"

I nod in return. I tap my backpack, where a sling of circular explosive disks lies.

"Alright," she says. "Let's go then."

I grab her hand, and the two of us run down the hallway. We make it to a set of stairs, and we climb them. We don't run into any guards as we move through another hall. They must be fighting somewhere else, likely against Thaxter. I hear more gunshots coming from above us, which just confirms that thought to me. I think we're almost there. If I remember correctly, the engine room is also on the east side.

We emerge out of another flight of stairs and into a wide room with tall ceilings. Buzzing and a mechanical grind noise comes from the other end of the space. The opposite wall from us is lined with massive domes turned on their sides, blue light radiating out of them. There are over ten of them in total, and control panels rest next to each of them. Steam curls out of large exhaust pipes on the ground, covering the room in haze.

I open my backpack and hand Skye two long slings of explosives. I start down the right side of the engines, and she heads down to the other end. I remove the first explosive and push down a yellow button on it. It beeps and hums, indicating that it's fully armed. I set it against the engine, and it sticks there. I continue this process twice on each engine and then until I reach Skye. I step back to see all of the engines. Each of them has two circular disks on them.

"We can go up to the top deck now," I say. "When we reach it, we'll get out of here with Thaxter and the others. As soon as we get in the air, I'll blow the charges, and this ship will sink."

Skye nods, and I lead us out of the room. We ascend another set of stairs and emerge into a hangar bay. Fighter jets line the entire hangar, and the black and white ghost logo of the Shadow Group is patterned along the hull of each jet. They're lined up in four rows along the front of the hangar, and each of them is being fueled. I climb a ladder, and this time we step onto the main deck.

As Skye reaches the top of the ladder, I immediately pull her to the left. Gunshots ricochet off of the ground around me, and I roll behind a wide metal power generator. I hear bullets clanging against the metal surface of the generator.

"Laurings' soldiers seem to have set up a perimeter around the deck," I shout. "Thaxter and the others are waiting on the right side of the deck. Right now, they're holding their position around the plane we used to get here. I'm going to have them set up a distraction that draws the fire away from us. Get ready to run."

Skye nods. I peek out from behind the power generator. The deck of the ship is a wide flat field of concrete that stretches for hundreds of yards. A boxy command tower is positioned in the center of the deck, and I can see lights flashing through its windows.

"Let's go," I say.

The two of us sprint to the right. A wave of bullets rushes towards us, though it's clear that there are only a few soldiers focused on us right now. I can see a fire erupting across the deck of the ship near the command center, and an explosion shakes the ground. Thaxter's distraction.

I hold up my left arm and tap my wristband. It expands into the round metal shield I've used many times before to defend myself. Skye activates hers too, and the sound of bullets echoing off the metal shields fills my ears. The force of the shots colliding against the shields slows me down as I run diagonally across the deck.

Thaxter spots us. His group of soldiers moves into the cargo plane. I pull a detonator from my backpack and push the red button on the top of it. A massive explosion rumbles from within the ship, and a loud groan comes from the deck. Laurings' soldiers are no longer focused on firing at us. The majority of them are moving below deck, where they're going to abandon this carrier. I see several lifeboats being dumped into the water from the side of the ship. Fighter jets are taking off from the main hangar bay, skimming across the water to avoid anti-aircraft missiles coming from other carriers.

I feel the ground slant below my feet, and the carrier groans from inside. I hear waves crash up against the deck, and the bottom left corner of the ship slams into the water, sending white columns of spray into the air. Skye and I make it to the cargo plane, and we stumble up the boarding ramp in a hurry. Thaxter and another soldier help us forward, and we catch our breath. The ramp folds up and into the plane behind us, and I feel the plane rising up from the deck. I rush to the windows. I see the carrier disappearing into the ocean, flames licking across the water, and clusters of debris rising and falling in the waves. I feel satisfied knowing that Laurings' attack on the NAIS in San Francisco is less likely now. Laurings himself is dead too.

I help Skye sit down on a bench to the side of the cargo hold. The bullet wound on her leg has started to become infected, but I think Thaxter will have someone to treat it.

Thaxter and one of his soldiers enter the main cargo hold of the plane and walk over to us. Thaxter sits down next to me.

"The American forces have launched a full-scale attack on the Shadow Group fleet," Thaxter says. "It's a good thing that we found you when we did."

He hands me a syringe, which I know is a painkiller. I inject it into my arm and wince. After several seconds the pain fades away to a mild throb. I nod my thanks to him.

"While I was on Laurings' carrier, he interrogated me. He had a plan to get the file's location from me," Skye says. "If I didn't give him the location, he threatened to have his forces attack the NAIS base in San Francisco. I think he was going to torture the location out of my father."

I cast her a worried glance. "Did you tell Laurings that we have the file? What happened to him after the ship was destroyed?"

Skye shakes her head. "I didn't tell him, and you both know I never would've."

Thaxter grunts in agreement.

"I managed to catch him off guard, and I fought him and four other soldiers. That's how I made it into the hallway and met you, August."

"Laurings is the type of person who can be over-confident and let down his guard when he thinks he has control of the situation." I lock eyes with her. "That's great work."

I hear shouts coming from the cockpit. Skye and Thaxter stand, both of them wanting to know what the commotion is about. Casey, one of the soldiers who'd accompanied us to the research facility earlier, runs to us. He can't even catch his breath.

"Our radio sensory arrays are picking up a group of fighter jets following us," he says. "They're from the NAIS, by the looks of it. What are your orders, sir?" He stares at Thaxter.

"Get the weapons systems of this plane online," Thaxter replies. "Have the entire crew equipped with gear for an emergency jump from the plane. Radio base and tell them we're going to try to make it back to them, whether it's using this plane or not. When the jets get within range and open fire, deploy all of our flares."

Casey nods. "If we're shot down, where should we aim to land with our chutes?"

Thaxter ponders that. His grizzled features and flat jawline condense as he thinks.

"There's an island lined with dense forests about a mile from here. If we can make it there, no amount of fire from the jets outside of heavy bombs will be able to force us into the open. And have base send a sub to pick us up from there."

Casey rushes away and passes Thaxter's orders to the others. I grab a parachute from a rack on the wall and bring it over. I help Skye slide her arms and legs into it. Once she's geared up, I pull one on for myself.

As I help Skye across the loading bay, the entire plane shakes. I lose my balance and crash into the wall, my shoulder colliding with two metal pipes. I shout in pain. The alarm starts to blare, indicating a missile lock on the plane. Over the wind outside, I hear pops coming from the plane's hull. Bullets are tearing through the plane.

Thaxter and the others have taken places along the walls, inside small rooms that represent the plane's weapon targeting systems. There's a console with a rotating chair that displays the plane's surroundings. Turrets on the plane's exterior will fire and turn in correspondence to what the people inside the targeting rooms do. All Thaxter is doing is delaying the collapse of the plane and creating time for us to jump off.

Thaxter's second in command, Denis, motions for everyone to gather around him. We do.

"Listen up," he says. "We've got fifteen seconds before this plane gets hit by a missile. On my count, I'm going to open the cargo bay door, and we're going to parachute out. Rendezvous at the south end of the island you see below us. Each of you should be equipped with a comms system."

He walks over to Skye and me and hands us each a pair of earbuds, one of them fitted with a mic.

"Good luck, soldiers," Denis tells us.

An explosion screams through the cargo bay, and the plane dips to the left. Fire erupts from the left side of us. Denis pushes a button on the wall, and the bay door folds down, revealing blue sky and clouds. I see a group of fighter jets racing toward us.

Skye grabs my hand and pulls me forward. In groups of two, the crew jumps out and tucks their arms behind them. Within seconds, it's our turn. I don't hesitate.

My feet leave the ground, and I jump off the end of the cargo bay. The wind whips through my hair, and my body feels light as I glide through the air. I pull my arms to my side and angle myself downwards.

The island that Thaxter and Denis mentioned comes into view. It's a wide expanse of land with mountains on the north side and densely packed trees dotting the south side. I hear the sound of jet engines rushing toward me. I'm confused. Aren't they supposed to be following Thaxter?

I crane my neck as I dive downward. Two of the jets from the original group are diving nose-down toward us. They're closing in much faster than we're moving. I glance down towards the island. It's much too early to pull our chutes.

I shout into my mic, but I can't even hear my own words over the roaring wind. No one else can hear me either. I'm going to be crushed by the planes if I don't do something. I yank the cord on my back, and the parachute deploys. My descent slows, and the sound of the engines rushes toward me. I pull my gun from its holster.

As the nearest jet closes in towards me, I aim my gun at my parachute. I pull the trigger, and the bullet rips through the fabric. I feel air rushing through the middle of the chute, and I feel myself falling without control. I look behind me, and the jet rushes next to me. I reach my arm out in midair, and I'm able to grab the jet's tail fin. It drags me down with it, and I position my foot under an air flap. I struggle to keep my body on the jet's hull.

Blood seeps from my hand from where I'd grabbed the sharp edge of the fin. I slowly work my way toward the cockpit, moving slowly to make sure I don't lose my grip. The island comes into view, barely a minute away. I have to make a move on the cockpit now.

I grip the gun tightly and fire it into the hinge that holds the cockpit down. It clangs against the metal, and I shift to the left. The cockpit blows off, and the entire windscreen flies backward and hits the tail fin before it falls downward away from the jet. The two pilots in the cockpit shout when they see me, and I send a bullet into each of them. I climb down the jet and into the cockpit, pushing them both out of the way and into the open air. I buckle myself into the front seat, the wind rushing against my face.

I take hold of the control yokes and push down on the jet's accelerator. The jet rushes downward, and I spot the other one. I watch in shock as its left wing slices through two soldiers, their blood spraying across the jet's hull. I push the jet to go faster, and when I'm within missile range of the other jet, I fire an entire magazine of tracker-locked missiles.

A compartment lying along the bottom of my jet opens and releases a volley of missiles. Their tails glow bright red as the warheads dart downward toward the jet I'd taken aim at. The missiles scream through the air and collide with the jet before the pilot has a chance to react. The jet goes up in flames, and debris scatters across the air. I swerve sharply to the right in order to avoid anything hitting my jet.

I breathe a sigh of relief. I let my jet slow down as the ground nears. I tap my mic and talk into it.

"This is August," I say. "I managed to hijack one of the jets that was following us. I'm above the island right now, and I'm about to land. Don't shoot; I'm friendly."

Denis' voice comes through. "Copy that, August. Land on the tall rock at the very south tip of the island. We'll see you there."

I loosen my seatbelts and lean over the edge of the jet, given that there's no windscreen anymore. I spot the rock that Denis had mentioned, which is really more like a giant slab of stone. I guide the jet inland and then make a turn back toward the rock. I turn the jet's nose downward and spot the rest of the group. I land the jet lightly, letting the landing gear fold out as I feel the jet touch down onto solid rock.

I unbuckle myself and slide out of the cockpit. I jump off the jet and land squarely on the rock. The others stand up and walk toward me. I search through the group. There are four fewer people here than we had earlier. Denis and Skye are left, as well as six others. The loss is disheartening.

"Do you know if Thaxter and the rest of the group made it off the plane?" I ask.

Skye shakes her head. "Still no word from them." She glances upward into the sky as if searching for the plane. "We saw an explosion thirty seconds ago, around two miles north and up in the sky. Let's hope that it wasn't them."

Denis nods from next to her. "We should get moving inland. Our base sent us a rendezvous point that's near the eastern side of the island. I don't want the NAIS to send a search party for us. We should move quickly."

Skye and I lead the way, with Denis bringing up the rear of the group. We head inland into the forests. Water drips from streams, and the occasional waterfall presents itself as we make our way along a path filled with bushes and fallen coconuts. Every rustle in the trees puts me on guard. The possibility that the NAIS did indeed send soldiers to look for us isn't completely out of the picture.

The path we've taken slants steeply upwards, and we begin walking alongside a long stream that weaves through rocks. When we're halfway through climbing up the side of a flat cliff wall, a shout echoes through the area below us.

I glance downwards, my hands clinging to the sharp vines of the cliff wall. Skye looks down from above us and motions for me to start moving down. The entire group makes it down to the bottom. I survey the bushes and trees around us, searching for where the shout may have come from. There's a cliff edge lining the side of the clearing we're in. I realize that Denis is nowhere to be seen. I take a glance around our group to see if anyone else is missing, but he's the only one that's not here.

I hear a rustle from the undergrowth to my left. Several seconds pass, and I unholster my gun. The others do the same, and they fan out around me. A deep, maniacal laugh comes from the bushes. It lasts for ten good seconds before a group of soldiers steps out into our sight, their guns raised. In the center of the group is Denis, with a gun held to his head. I recognize the person holding the gun behind him. It's the armored soldier that's continued to attack Skye and me. But this time, we know who's under the mask.

FIFTEEN

The first instinct I have when I see Hunter is to raise my gun and fire. But right now, that's not an option. There's more of them than there are of us, and if we try to reach for our weapons, we'll be shot dead before we take aim. Even so, as I stare into Hunter's masked face, I feel anger surge through my veins. I thought he was my friend, my best friend. But, in fact, he's a murderer working with Laurings.

"Hand over the file, August," Hunter shouts from twenty meters away.

The sound of my name on his lips enrages me further. He presses the barrel of his gun harder against Denis' temple when I don't reply.

"You're surrounded," he adds, shoving Denis forward a foot or so. "I'd hate to kill you, August. We've known each other for so long."

This isn't Hunter, not the Hunter I know. What did Laurings do to him? Has he been undercover this entire time?

No one replies. All of them, save for Skye, know that Thaxter and I made a false copy of the file before we came to rescue her. The real one is resting in a warehouse, heavily protected by guards.

"I'll give you a minute before I start shooting," Hunter says.

The others in our group look to me for what to do. I can feel the gaze of Hunter's soldiers on my back. What is so important about this file that it's worth going to such lengths over? I remember that several weeks ago, after a mission in Ewen, I learned that Laurings had obtained File 337. There was a rumor back at my base in California that File 337 was connected to File 338, the one I have right now. What was the phrase they had used? I think they were twin files, meaning that one can't be opened without the other. They must have something extremely important on them.

I open my pant pocket and pull out the file. The soldiers step forward, their guns trained on me. I hope the others notice this. I walk forward, drawing everyone's attention. I stop ten feet away from Hunter. He smiles.

"So you've made a choice?" Hunter says. "Good, good."

I nod. "There's no point in fighting a fight you can't win. At least, most of the time." I show him the file, and his smile grows into a grin. "Take it, but leave our group unharmed."

"Thank you," he says.

I place the file on the grass in front of him. He bends down to pick it up, and my hand moves to my gun. The soldiers see this, but not after I've ducked. I roll across the grass in front of the file and fire my gun at it. It shatters into a thousand fragments of metal and glass. Hunter's eyes widen, and he freezes. I send a bullet into his chest.

I snake forward and send my leg into his stomach. The collision sends his body flying backward, and he tumbles over the edge of the cliff. My breath catches in my throat as I watch his body fall downwards. I see it hit the ocean below, the collision sending up columns of water high into the air.

I hear guns firing, but I'm unharmed. I stand slowly and shakily. My heart beats so fast that I swear I can hear it. All around me, Hunter's soldiers are lying on the grass, dead and filled with bullets. Across the clearing, the rest of my group walks over to me. They're holding their guns in their hands. Skye gives me a pat on the back.

"Good plan," she says. "But was destroying the file the only way?"

I shake my head. "When you were on Laurings' flagship, Thaxter and I made a copy of the file. The real one's nowhere near us."

She laughs, a beautiful sound. "Thank god."

She pulls me in for a hug, and I welcome her embrace. I still haven't thought more about when I'm going to tell her about how I feel. The thought that she doesn't feel the same way scares me.

I pull away and look over the edge of the cliff. Hunter's body isn't there anymore. It's probably under the water. Part of me knows that his death is a good thing, but another remembers the childhood friend that's been on hundreds of missions with me. Right now, he's lying on the ocean floor. And I'm the one that shot him.

The sound of engines nears. I look at the sky and am dismayed to see a large military plane flying toward us. A fighter jet flanks it on either side, and all three ships have the Shadow Group symbol emblazoned on them. They're Hunter's backup.

I turn to the rest of the group. Denis is thankfully still alive and unharmed.

"We need to go."

Denis nods. "There's an inlet of water near the center of the island. It's deep, so the sub will be waiting for us there. If we can make it onto the sub, we'll be safe to return back to base." He locks eyes with me. "It'll be better if we split up; that way, we draw less attention."

"Alright. I'll take Skye and three others along the west side, through the trees. We'll meet you at the inlet. Good luck."

I lead our group of five toward the side of the clearing we had entered.

FIFTEEN

The inlet is still the same way we were heading initially, and I see that Denis has sent up a flare to the south, likely as a distraction for the jets. I begin climbing the rock wall, my arms and legs moving with a sense of urgency. When we reach the top, I take one last look at the water that Hunter fell in. The sight sends a pang of guilt through my body. I turn away, knowing that dwelling on his death isn't going to help us get off of this island.

Still, knowing that I've killed Hunter chills me to the bone.

SIXTEEN

Fortunately for us, the path leading to the inlet is completely devoid of anything other than lush green plants and towering trees. We cross over the top of a small ridge, and down below us lies a long stretch of crystal blue water. It snakes into the land in a long river that juts out as far as I can see. At the end of it must lie the open ocean.

I spot Denis' group emerging from the cover of the palm trees, but they're moving much faster than us. I watch from the top of the ridge as Denis and two others run into the clearing, sweat pouring down their faces. Blood is smeared across their cheeks, and they pant in exhaustion. Where's the other member of their group? They must've been attacked by Laurings' soldiers.

Just on cue, gunshots echo from the forest. I hear a bloodcurdling scream and rustling in the undergrowth. I motion to Skye and the other three soldiers in our group. We run down the steep slope of sand into the inlet. I hear water gurgling from in front of us, and the black metal hull of a submarine slowly emerges from beneath the surface of the water. The inlet must be very deep for the submarine to get so close to us. I run along the left side of it, meeting with Denis.

"Where's Atusha?" I ask him.

Denis pants hard, his chest rising and falling rapidly. A long cut runs down the side of his face, stretching all the way to his neck. I have no idea what could have caused that.

"She got stuck behind us. We couldn't stop."

I nod, sending a silent prayer to her. "Let's get inside the sub."

The side of the submarine opens, and a stepladder drops out and onto the sand. Skye goes up first with the others. Denis and I wait behind and then climb up and into the submarine. Denis runs down the hallway we've climbed down into. I stay on the edge, my eyes scanning the tree line for any sign of Atusha. I'll do anything I can to not leave somebody behind.

I see her emerge from the bushes on the right. I shout to her to run faster. As she's around twenty yards out from the submarine, a bullet flashes across the clearing and strikes her in the forehead. I immediately duck down into the hallway and press a button on the wall. The door in the wall that had opened earlier now closes. Atusha is dead. There's nothing I can do about that.

I make my way down the hall. White lights line either side of the hallway, illuminating the space around me. The hallway opens up into a massive command room. There's a huge domed window at the end of it, blue water showing through the clear glass. Three steps lead up to a diamond-shaped space enclosed by a metal railing. Consoles and computers encircle the area. Denis, Skye, and the others are waiting next to the hub. Inside the hub itself are crew members, each of them wearing blue overalls with red stripes on them. Some of them are sitting before monitors, others working levers and speed meters. None look up as I come in.

I feel the submarine moving through the water, and I can faintly hear gunshots. Bullets fly into the water in front of us, visible through the window. They plunge into the inlet but slow down as they hit the surface. I feel the ground slant underneath me, and the nose of the submarine tilts down. This inlet is surprisingly deep. The submarine dives down and speeds up, the propellers roaring loudly even though they're at the back of the ship.

"We're on our way to the Big Island," one of the crew members says.

He's a tall man with a neatly trimmed beard and dark brown eyes. He doesn't wear overalls like the others, but rather a navy blue jacket. There's a badge pinned to the jacket that shows that he's the captain of this vessel.

Denis crosses the room to me. His eyes look haunted by the journey here. He's probably thinking about how Atusha died. But there was nothing anybody could've done short of them being killed as well.

"There's something I have to tell you, August," Denis says.

He puts a hand on my arm and pulls me away from the others into the hallway that I came from.

"Thaxter told me that if ever he was missing, I was to give you this information. No one outside of our group can know what I'm about to tell you, is that clear?"

I nod. "I won't say anything," I tell him.

"Good," Denis replies. "As you know, the file we recovered from the NAIS facility is being kept in a safe house in Honolulu. There's no way that Laurings can find it short of torturing the location tracker out of the director." He looks me in the eye. "We believe that if we can retrieve the second file, we'll be able to access what's inside both of them. Thaxter believes that the files are connected to Project Rising Star."

I feel my eyebrows jump up. Project Rising Star is the most classified project in the NAIS.

Denis continues. "If we can access what's inside, we'll have the answers to everything that's going on with our agency. Right now, it's corrupt because too many people are guarding this project. Obtaining File 337 could be the final piece of this mad puzzle."

I try to comprehend everything that Denis is telling me. I know that we have the second file, number 338. Its twin, number 337, is something we can get too. He's right—if we're able to connect the two files together, it's possible that many of our questions about the NAIS secrets will be answered.

"Alright," I say. "But doesn't Laurings have possession of the file right now?"

He shakes his head. "There were reports that an NAIS Black-ops team retrieved the file from Laurings' flagship after we rescued Skye. The NAIS has it back now."

"How do we find it then? There are hundreds of places it could be right now."

Denis nods. "I read the NAIS file on Skye. She's well known to be an extremely gifted hacker. It's possible that she could run a hack on the file we do have, and it could lead us to find out where the other file is." He glances back towards the command room, where we can see the water shimmering through the massive window. "Once we get to the Big Island, we'll get to our base in the city of Honolulu. Skye can run some hacks on the file, and if we do find it, then we'll gear up and make our way to the file. It won't be an easy mission, but I believe that it's doable."

"That sounds like a plan," I say. "Let's get that file."

Sweat drips down my back as I make my way through a mall on the west side of Honolulu. Skye and the others walk with me, all of them exhausted from the heat of the sun as well. Thaxter's base is supposedly here in the city, right in the middle of a mall. It's different from the one I'd been brought to after the file extraction. I'm not sure what to expect, given that it must be concealed within the buildings around us.

Denis leads us to the corner of the mall, directly underneath a towering skyscraper that winds up into the sky. We enter the building through a tall glass archway at the front of it. We walk across the building's main lobby and towards the elevators. Denis pushes a button on the wall, and an elevator greets us, its doors sliding open.

When we're inside, Denis moves to the panel with buttons representing different floors. I watch intently as his fingers move across the panel, pressing multiple buttons. Seven, thirteen, sixty, eighty-three. He continues pressing buttons that seem random, but I know they must be part of some type of special passcode. Denis doesn't stop until he's pressed at least twenty buttons. When he's finished, the elevator begins to move upwards.

After some time, the elevator stops, and a screen that indicates what level we're on shows ninety-three. I glance at the panel of buttons. Ninety-three isn't a level that's accessible on the panel. Neither are ninety-four, five, and six. These four levels must be where Denis is taking us.

The doors slide open, and our group steps into a hallway lit with bright bulbs hanging from the ceilings. Two guards are waiting inside the hallway, and they lead us down it. We emerge into a massive room with floor-to-ceiling windows stretching across three of the four walls. The view shows the expanse of the city, the surrounding skyscrapers equally as tall as the room we're in. A glass spiral staircase twists upwards from the left side of the room and leads up into the next level.

Denis sits down in the corner of the room, where three wide couches lie. He presses his thumb against the armrest, and a table emerges from the ground. Resting atop the table are three tall computer monitors. Skye and I join him on the couches while the others in our group climb the spiral staircase. I wonder what's on the levels above us.

"We're going to retrieve the file from the warehouse," Denis tells Skye and me. "Normally I would have our soldiers there bring it, but we've heard reports of NAIS forces inside the city."

I narrow my eyes. There are a lot of reservations I have about Thaxter's soldiers. I should ask now before we get too deep into this.

"Denis, does Thaxter have some sort of secret organization outside of the NAIS?" I ask. "Because I'm having some trouble understanding how so many NAIS soldiers would abandon the agency and just follow your orders."

Denis nods at me. "I understand. The truth is, we haven't told you nearly as much as we should have. One year ago, when Thaxter first learned about Taylor's disloyalty to the NAIS, he asked me to help him recruit some of the agents he knew to create a small group. Those soldiers that helped you back at the facility, those who manned the submarine, and those with us now are all part of that group."

"So when you learned that the agency is corrupt, did you bring together the soldiers that we're with now?" Skye asks.

"Precisely," Denis replies. "We needed a team that we could trust to help us on our missions. The soldiers we have are some of the NAIS' best."

"Alright," I say. "When are we going to retrieve the file from the warehouse?"

Denis types into one of the monitors. He seems to be sending a message to someone.

"We're going to go now, actually. Once we get there, we'll come back, and Skye, you can try to hack into it to find the location."

She nods. I told her about the plan back in the submarine, and she said she was up to it. I'm really glad that she is. It just makes me admire her more, and it also makes it harder to ignore my feelings. I'm going to have to tell her at some point; I'm just not sure when the right time is.

"I should be able to hack through the main firewall of the file in order to access the encrypted location of the other file," Skye tells us. "It won't be hard, but it'll take some time to get the information we need."

Denis stands up. "We'll take two cars to the warehouse and come back as quickly as we can. I don't want us to have any trouble getting back here."

Four of the soldiers that had gone upstairs now come back down. Each of them is dressed in a black vest outfitted with different explosives and guns. One is carrying two additional vests and hands them to Skye and me.

I pull mine on top of my jumpsuit and make sure it fits tightly. This seems like a lot of gear to be using for a simple warehouse visit. There must be serious concern from Denis and the others that there are NAIS soldiers inside Honolulu. It would make sense that they are, though. If Laurings' forces are still in Hawaii, then the NAIS would probably want to have soldiers inside of the major cities.

"Ready?" Denis asks Skye and me. He's wearing a vest of his own, and he gives each of us a pistol and a set of earbuds. I realize that he's hefting a shotgun in his hands. It's an unconventional weapon in the modern day, but if that's his weapon of choice, then who am I to judge?

I nod, and Skye does too. Denis leads us and the four other soldiers back into the elevator where he presses another series of buttons. We stop on the fourteenth floor. The elevator doors open into a garage, where two cars are waiting. I notice that they're different models, and one of them is red while the other is black. The rest of the garage is empty aside from another car in the corner. A gated entrance is on the far side of the garage.

"Skye and August, you'll ride with Tanner and me," Denis tells us.

I follow him to the second car, where Skye and I sit in the back seats. The engine starts, and the car begins to move. I see the gate at the end of the garage roll up and into the ceiling. The car in front of us drives down a long ramp that leads to the street. We follow it.

Once we get down to the street level, we drive along a smaller road separate from the larger ones. As we're driving, Skye leans forward and rolls up a glass divider in the middle of the car that separates the front and back seats. She looks at me.

"Are you alright, August?" Skye asks, her eyes searching my face. "I know that Hunter's death must be hard for you, but it was something that you couldn't avoid."

I nod at her. "I'm fine, I guess," I reply. "It's just that I knew Hunter for so long, and knowing that he's dead because of me is … hard to take in."

She puts a hand on my shoulder. Her touch feels good, and I'm grateful for this moment.

"It's not your fault that he wasn't who we thought he was," Skye tells me. "I'm here for you if you need anything."

"Thanks," I say. "That means a lot to me."

The rest of the drive is spent in silence. We drive for half an hour before we reach an abandoned district. There's a wide blue warehouse at the end of the street we're on. Both cars stop, and we get out of them.

My eyes scan the street around us. It's rather deserted, and the warehouse is surrounded by nothing but junkyards with scraps of old metal in them. I follow Denis as our group makes our way to the front of the warehouse. Its metal walls are covered in peeling blue paint, and rust has formed on the majority of the building. I look for an entrance but see none other than the massive steel-grated face of the warehouse. My guess is that it lifts upwards.

"Wait here," Denis says.

He steps forward to the front of the warehouse, and the rest of us watch from ten feet away. He taps on the metal three times with his fist. A scanner pops out from the wall and extends to reach Denis. Denis kneels, and the scanner flashes a green light across his eyes. He then places his finger on the device, and it blinks green again.

I hear a rumbling sound from the warehouse, and its front door heaves up from the ground. We wait for ten seconds as it lifts up and into the warehouse's roof. Four guards are waiting inside for us, and they hurriedly usher us inside. I run inside, and the door closes behind us.

I survey the space around me. The warehouse is almost cavernous to me, and its main body stretches farther than I can see. I can make out rows and rows of boxes stacked high onto shelving units.

"This way," Denis tells us.

Skye, Tanner, and I follow him while the rest of the group waits with the guards at the front door. They all seem to be on guard as if soldiers are going to barge through the door any second.

Denis leads us down an aisle in the middle of the warehouse between two tall rows of shelves. I crane my neck to see what's inside the boxes. I'm surprised to see that they're full of guns and explosives. What do Thaxter and Denis need all of these weapons for?

We stop near the end of the file. Denis bends over and reaches up to one of the shelves. He pulls out a black box with a velvet border on it. It looks identical to some of the other boxes in the warehouse, but I doubt that the file is in it. As he opens it with a press of his thumb, I realize that I'm correct. Inside is a tiny silver key.

"What's that for?" I ask Denis.

He looks up at me. "You'll see," he replies. "We went through some unique security measures to protect the file. We would've done something different if we'd had more time."

I nod and follow him as he leads us down another aisle. We stop, this time about halfway through, where Denis kneels down once more. He pushes aside a group of boxes that hold grenades in them. I watch as he pulls on a handle that's protruding from the ground. It turns and pulls upwards, revealing a small compartment in the ground. Inside that is a safe door, which is facing up. He presses his hand against a reader on the door's face. Denis inserts the key in a small hole In the door. The safe clicks, and the door unlocks. Denis pulls it up and inside lies the file.

He nods at me, and I bend down next to him. I reach inside the safe and pull out the file. It comes out easily, and I stare at it for a second, still surprised that so many people are fighting for control of this small thing. The file looks exactly the same as it had when I'd last seen it.

A voice comes through my earbuds. It's distressed and sounds urgent. "Denis, there's a Shadow Group helo coming—"

The sound of gunfire follows, and the transmission ends abruptly. I hear an explosion, and when I turn to see the front of the building, it's lit with flames. More gunshots come from the front, coupled with shouts from soldiers. I can't tell if that's our soldiers or the Shadow Group's.

A different voice comes on. "Denis, there's too many of them. You need to get out of—"

Again, the voice cuts out abruptly. I glance at Denis for a second, and our group of four takes off, running in the opposite direction of the front door. We need to get out of here before they find us. The file is too important, and we can't just leave it in Denis' safe.

How could the Shadow Group know where we are? It's possible that they have forces inside the city as well, but then how could they know that we were in the city in the first place? Not all of this adds up. There's something that we're missing here.

When we reach the end of the next aisle, we find the back wall of the warehouse. Two red alarms on the wall are blaring loudly, signaling that the warehouse has been breached. Denis takes us to a metal door on the wall, opens it, and ushers us through. Gunshots are still audible even as we step outside.

"We can't make it back to the cars." We continue running away from the warehouse until we've made it to one of the junkyards I'd seen earlier. "If we can find any type of transport, we need to make it as far away from here as we can."

Denis nods. "These junkyards must have something we can use. We'll split into two groups to search for a car. Hotwire it if you need to, and radio to us when you find something."

Tanner and I move to the left side of the junkyard while Skye and Denis take the other side. I pull a long knife from my belt and carve a large hole in the barbed wire fence that surrounds the junkyard. We step through and move through the area. I slam the knife into the head of a security camera we come across, sending sparks flying across the pebbly ground. My eyes scan the piles of scrap, looking for anything we can use. As we make it to the back of the junkyard, I realize we're walking through shut-down old cars. Tanner sees this, too, and we both try to find a car that looks like it could still run.

Most of them have been stripped for their parts, but I find a truck in the corner of the junkyard that looks newer. I stab my knife into the window, and it shatters. I put my hand inside and pull on the door handle, then slide my body underneath the dashboard and open up a panel to hotwire the engine. After several seconds of tinkering, the engine sputters to life.

I tap my earbud and turn on my mic. "I found a truck. It's on the southwest end of the yard."

Denis and Skye are here in half a minute. We all climb into the truck, and I slam down on the accelerator. I look for an exit to the junkyard, but all I see is the same barbed wire fence. I ram the truck into the fence. It blows apart with a screeching sound.

Our truck emerges onto a wide street dotted with cars moving up and down the lanes. I turn to Denis in the back seat.

"Where do we go?" I ask him. "The entire city's probably going to be swarming with Shadow Group soldiers, so I don't think that we can count anywhere as safe. And why was it so easy for them to ambush us?"

"There's no way they could've known about us," he tells me.

I turn back to face the truck's wheel, and I keep my eyes on the road as Denis continues.

"After you and Skye took down Laurings' flagship, I expected the Shadow Group to be less aggressive in their moves. I'm still not sure how they're tracking us, but our priority right now is just to make it out of the city. We can worry about making it to a safe house after."

I give him a nod in assent. He brings up a good point.

Before I have a chance to reply to Denis, an array of muzzle flashes show in the rearview mirror. The glass on the truck's rear windshield shatters, and so do the side rearview mirrors. I hear gunshots ricocheting off of our truck, and I duck down in my seat as bullets begin tearing the cushions of my seat apart.

Skye's craning her neck and looking back at the cars behind us. "I'm counting four cars tailing us," she shouts over the sound of the bullets. "All Shadow Group and heavily armed."

The car shakes as more gunshots drive holes into the tailgate. I smell gas coming from below me, and I know we're pushing the truck too fast. I see flames licking at the hood of the truck. It's only a matter of time before one of the oncoming bullets strike one of the truck's gas pipes, and I know we only have so much longer before the truck stops running.

"Fire back!" I yell over the loud ringing of the gunshots.

Skye and Tanner both roll down what's left of their windows and fire shots back at the cars behind us. I look up at the rearview mirror hanging above my head, and I spot the four cars Skye was talking about. All of them are sleek black, and one of them, much larger, has a soldier climbing up onto the roof from a hole in the car's center section. I hear a noise that's too familiar to me, and I see the front barrels of a mini-gun beginning to protrude from the roof of the car.

As the whir of the mini-gun starts, I take a hard right onto the freeway. I feel the truck's bumper jerk up and then down again as it hits the curb. In the mirror, I see the cars turn to follow us. I need to do something before that min-gun blows this car into a thousand pieces.

I look at our surroundings. Mountains lie in front of us, looming hundreds of feet above the freeway. There will be tunnels coming from up ahead of us that lead to the northern end of the island. Tunnels mean cover, which is something we could certainly use right now.

The sound of the mini-gun beginning to fire drowns out all of the other noises around me. I feel the entire truck being jolted forward as a group of bullets slam into the body of the car. I weave in between traffic, trying to avoid the mini-gun. I hear Tanner cry out in pain, and when I turn to see him, his entire chest has been ripped open from a bullet, and he's lying on the floor of the car, making not a single noise.

Most of the people on the freeway behind us have stopped their cars and are running out of the road. I spot a massive oil tanker truck merging onto the freeway ahead of us, and when the driver sees the commotion between us and the rest of the cars, he bails as well. Only his vehicle has so much weight on it that it slows down almost immediately, and I swerve left to avoid being smashed.

Skye takes the opportunity, and once we're ten meters away from the tanker, she fires on the massive tank of oil that it's carrying. Bullets pierce the metal shell, and the boom of an explosion sends waves of heat flying toward us. I look up at the mirror and watch as the tanker flips over from the explosion and the massive semi rams into one of the Shadow Group cars. The soldiers inside don't have time to get out before they're completely crushed.

I realize that another one of the black cars has been turned into a skeleton of itself, its metal frame charred and ablaze with flames. No one's inside, and fire is erupting from its roof. It must've been hit directly by the explosion of gas.

The largest car is still chasing us. The whir of its mini-gun begins again, and I know that this time, our truck won't survive a round of its heavy bullets. I turn my attention back to the road, and I see a tunnel coming up ahead of us. But that's the least of my worries. As I glance outside the window, I can see a black helicopter nearing us from the far left, its rotor blades spinning quickly toward us.

"Damn, a helicopter and a mini-gun? This is becoming too much for me," I say over the gunfire. I switch lanes, and the truck rams into another car.

I try to see if the driver I'd hit is okay, and Skye shouts, "He's fine."

I'm glad that the driver isn't hurt.

The dark tunnel nears, and I see a long line of cars waiting at a group of toll booths. They're all going to be decimated by the mini-gun if I don't draw the fire away.

I spot a path leading off from the side of the freeway. I don't see any road, and I notice a sign that reads HAZARD. I switch lanes again and head in that direction. What hazard could possibly be worse than a mini-gun?

I slam into the sign, and it flies upward and over the roof. The truck's wheels fly up and off the ground for several seconds before they slam onto a rocky road that winds downward. At the end of the path, I spot a cliff edge, and a wave of concern rushes through me. Skye throws me a questionable look.

The mini-gun begins to fire rounds at us, and Denis shouts for me to turn. I do as he says, and I veer into the dense forest of pine trees to my left, narrowly avoiding a trip off of the cliff. The mini-gun's bullets tear into the trees around us, sending leaves and bark flying across the front windshield. Fortunately, the denseness of the forest provides good momentary cover from the two cars behind us.

But I've failed to remember the chopper above us. I hear it nearing us, and the sound of rotors tearing through trees echoes across the forest. I again defer to the rearview mirror above me, and I see a rope ladder being lowered from the chopper's hull. A soldier climbs down and aims a rocket launcher at us.

I push down harder on the accelerator, but ninety miles an hour is as fast as this old thing will go. I can already hear the engine beginning to sputter out.

"Incoming!" Denis shouts.

I brace myself. The missile hits the ground almost directly behind the truck's rear bumper. The entire tail end of the truck is thrust upwards, and my face slams against the dash, and I feel blood leaking from my nose. The truck teeters to the left and almost tips over into a tree. I barely manage to regain control and straighten the truck.

The car with the mini-gun catches up to us on my right side.

"The mini-gun's out of rounds," Skye says next to me.

The soldier on the roof points a rifle at us and begins firing. Denis and Skye both duck down into their seats. When the soldier has used his clip, Denis pulls his shotgun from his belt and cocks it. I hear him opening his door, and a nearby pine tree breaks it clean off of its hinge. A loud blast erupts from behind me as a massive bullet slams straight into the soldier's chest.

As Denis is reloading the shotgun, Skye fires a round of bullets toward the car as well. Some of them manage to penetrate the window next to the driver's seat, and a bullet catches the driver in the shoulder. I hear him shout out, and I turn the truck towards that car. I jerk the steering wheel hard to the right and sideswipe the other car. The impact pushes the car away from us, and it skids straight into a tree trunk. The massive pine splits the car in two, and both sides erupt in an explosion.

The chopper closes in on us again. Another soldier climbs down the ladder, holding the reloaded rocket launcher.

"You've got to be kidding me," Denis says. "How many weapons do these assholes have?"

As the missile head emerges from the barrel of the launcher once more, I take my hands off the wheel and slide half of my body out of the window. I barely have time to aim before I pull the trigger on my gun. My bullet pierces straight into the body of the oncoming missile, and it explodes twenty meters away from me. I hear another explosion come, and when I slide back inside the truck, I see that the missile exploded near enough to the chopper that it hit it. The sound of tearing pines returns as the chopper veers out of control, its rotors cutting into the nearby trees. The fuselage slams into the trunk of a pine, and the impact creates a dent in the helo's main cabin. Another groan comes, and two of the rotor blades split off the helo's roof. The tear causes the chopper to be unbalanced, and as a result, its nose turns downward, and it flies straight down toward the ground. As it hits the grassy forest floor, it explodes and rips into pieces. Shards of metal fly and both the chopper itself and its rotors spring outward and hit the surrounding trees. I swerve the truck as the end of one of the rotors slams into a tree barely a foot next to me.

My eyes turn upwards to the rearview mirror. Where has the last Shadow Group car gone? I look out of Skye's window and then mine. I finally see the sleek black car pulling away from us and driving back up the hill. Two of the doors have flown off, and the rear bumper is completely torn off. It must've been damaged when the chopper exploded. Either they've been ordered back by the Shadow Group command, or they've just run. If it's the latter, I doubt they'll survive very long before the Shadow Group kills them for betrayal.

Next to me, Skye is breathing hard. So is Denis. I realize that I've been so concentrated on the chase that I haven't been breathing very much. My chest feels weak, and I stop the truck in a clearing. I feel bruises along my neck and forehead from the different bumps and hits the truck took.

The fresh air outside of the truck feels good as I push open my door. I rush to the back of the truck and open the left door. Inside lies Tanner, his chest still ripped open from the mini-gun round that he took. Blood stains his shirt and soaks the cushioned seats around him. Denis helps me pull him off of the floor, and the weight of his dead body feels two times heavier than it should be. Denis and I move him to the middle of the clearing, where we lay him flat on the forest floor. Skye joins us, and we all hang our heads in respect. While I hadn't known Tanner very long at all, he was an honorable and loyal person who fought hard for the right cause. It's horrible that he's joining countless other soldiers who've died from fighting the Shadow Group.

We each bend down and begin making a grave five feet to Tanner's right. It's a rough grave, and we don't spend much time on it—but it would be wrong not to properly bury him. Once the hole is dug, we gently lay Tanner inside and cover him with dirt. I take my finger and trace along the muddy ground, writing TANNER. Denis bends down and writes his last name, LONGHORN. I press my watch and make a mental note of the GPS coordinates we're at. If we ever get through all of this, it'll be nice to let Tanner's family know where he's buried. My heart fills with guilt and sorrow at the thought of telling his loved ones that he's dead.

I shake my head. Tanner was a good soldier, and he'd want us to move on. If he were here, he'd tell us to get moving. The Shadow Group could be doing something significant right now. I stand up and nod my head once more to the grave. I turn to face the truck to inspect the damage to it, to see whether it's still usable or not. Skye and Denis both join me.

The truck's front bumper looks to be damaged from when I hit the curb, and both of the front rearview mirrors are gone. One of the back tires is slightly flat, and the door Thaxter broke off is nowhere to be seen. The back of the truck is the worst. The rear windshield is nothing but a skeleton, bits and pieces of glass scattered across the inside and outside of the truck. A part of the trunk has torn off, a good long piece of metal just gone. Bullet holes dot the rest of the trunk, each of them close to the size of a golf ball. Whatever rounds that mini-gun used were massive. I take a look at the rear bumper, which is beginning to fall off. I take my knife and cut it off cleanly. And finally, I kneel on the ground and look at the underside of the truck. Two of the pipes are leaking gas, and three more are badly torn from the rough ride we had. There's no way to really patch them, but for now, I wrap a piece of metal wire tightly around each one of the leaking ones, creating a noose around them to stop the flow of the oil.

When I'm done, I stand up and nod at Skye and Denis. Denis climbs into the backseat, and Skye and I climb into the front of the car. I inspect the fuel meter, and to my dismay, there are only about thirty miles left in this thing. I should be grateful that there is anything in this car at all—it's old, and at the junkyard, it was probably about to be stripped for its parts. That, coupled with the leaking pipes, are the reasons why we won't be able to get too far with what's left in the truck's tank.

"That was some great driving back there," Skye says as I pull on my seatbelt. "A lot of great decision-making," she adds.

"Thanks," I reply. "Likewise with you two. It wasn't easy getting out of that situation."

I duck under the dash and quickly get the engine going by sparking two wires together. When I come back up, Skye's leaning forward with her hands on the dash. That's when I see the tracker.

I see it on the inside of Skye's sleeve, embedded in the wavy blue fabric of her shirt, woven in so that it doesn't touch her skin. The device itself is almost too small to make out. It's a minute black chip with a faint red hue emerging from the center of it. Even though someone on the street might say that it's something else, I know without a doubt that it is a tracking device.

"Skye," I say. She turns towards me. "There's a tracker on you."

She frowns. "A tracker?" She looks around at her body. "Where is it?"

I can tell by the confusion on her face that she genuinely didn't know about it. That's either good for us, or she's a great actor, and then we're definitely screwed. I'll go with the first option. I can't bear the thought that Skye's a double agent and was tracking herself so that the Shadow Group could find us.

I hold her hand and turn it over. She sees it on the inside of her sleeve and nods at me. When she pulls it off and looks at it closely, she hands it to me.

"It's definitely a tracker." Skye pauses. "They must've put it on me when I was unconscious aboard Laurings' flagship."

"That makes complete sense," Denis says. "That's how the Shadow Group has been following us all of this time." He nods at me, an indication for me to destroy it.

I hold the tiny device in my hand. I pull my knife from my belt and put my hand outside the window. When I'm sure that the pieces will fall outside of the truck, I stab the handle of the knife down onto the tracker. It erupts in a small shower of sparks, and bits and pieces of glass fall to the ground.

"Where to now?" I ask Denis. "We still need to find the other file, don't we?"

"We do," he says. "And in order for us to do that, Skye needs a computer, correct?" When Skye nods at him, he continues. "Alright then, we'll continue to my safe house outside of the city. I don't know exactly where we are now, but if we follow the freeway for around twenty miles, we should be near it."

"Sounds like a plan," I say.

I press the accelerator, and the truck slowly begins to move forward. I can feel the damage that was done to this already dilapidated truck. I turn the truck around and head back in the direction we came.

As I look through the woods ahead of us, it's clear that something went down here. An entire path has been carved through the forest, a result of the mini-gun and the chopper. Dozens of trunks lie flat on the ground, and flames are spreading from the different explosions we caused. The entire forest may burn, but whatever is in the file is far more important than that. I just wouldn't want to be the person who has to explain this to the government.

And even if I was that person, I'd have no clue how to.

SEVENTEEN

Once we reach the freeway, police cars are making their way down the open road in the direction of the forest. Civilian cars are parked along the freeway, and people are on their phones instead of driving. Some of them are even yelling at officers, complaining about the damage to their cars.

As we continue down the freeway, no one pays us any attention. We follow a group of cars that have decided to continue down the wide road. I do as Denis had instructed and drive down the freeway for roughly fifteen miles. I see that the mountains have faded away behind us, and the humid part of Hawaii has returned.

"Here," Denis says from behind me.

He points at the exit, and I take it, driving the car up a winding ramp and onto a more secluded road. The road is lined by palm trees on either side, a sharp contrast to the pines back in the more mountainous area.

A group of colorful houses with triangular-shaped roofs make up the abundance of the buildings that line the sidewalk. Denis points at one of them near the middle of the street, and I stop the truck. Opening the door and stepping outside onto the sidewalk, I notice immediately that the building looks identical to most of the others. Just like the hideout in the city, it blends in by being completely ordinary.

Denis leads us to the front of the building, which I would identify as a house. We walk up three stairs and onto the front porch, where Denis pulls a key from his pocket and inserts it into the lock on the front door. It clicks, and the door opens with a creak.

I'm taken aback when I see the first room we emerge into. I would've expected to see a quaint living room, but instead, I step into a space with polished metal walls and no furniture. The room looks just like a prison cell, with no visible exit and nothing lying about. Denis shuts the door behind us.

"Is this some type of entrance?" I ask as I continue to examine my surroundings.

"Precisely," Denis replies.

He walks to the left side of the room, where he pushes on a random place on the wall. Surprisingly the section of metal that he touches moves outward towards him, and out comes a tray with a hand scanner on it. Denis places his palm on the screen, and it flashes green. He steps back to stand next to Skye and me. There's a pause.

I feel my feet drop slightly, and when I look down, I see that the floor space we're standing on has begun to lower into the ground. When we've descended several meters, two metal panels join together to block our view of the room above. My guess is that we're in some type of elevator, and the floor that just closed above us is part of the system. Where we're going is unknown to me.

The ground stops moving downward shortly after it starts. We stop in another metal room, but this time the wall in front of us is open, and it leads into a massive underground space that's too large to be called a room. The cavernous space is filled with racks of weapons, tables, and computer monitors. I even see a car hiding in the shadows on the opposite end.

"Welcome to Hideout Alpha," Denis says.

"Looks like Thaxter had a plan for everything," I say.

"This is Thaxter's primary backup hideout on the island, meaning that if the location in the city was compromised, then this is the first place he would come," Denis tells me.

He strides across the room over to the computers, and I see Skye's eyes light up at the sight. It should be more than enough for her to hack the files, especially considering how proficient she is with technology.

"This is perfect," Skye says as she sits down in front of a desk with a computer on it.

"The passcode is—" Denis begins, but Skye's already opened the computer.

I chuckle to myself. I walk over to her and pull the file from my pocket, and then hand it to her. She takes it and places it on a circular device which pulls the file inside of it. Within a second, blue lines of code are running across Skye's screen.

"August," Denis calls from across the space. "Let's get some gear ready for when Skye finds where the other file is."

I nod and jog over to him. He takes me to the side of the space where most of the weapons are. I see two hangers that would normally be for jackets and sweaters but are holding dozens of Kevlar vests in this case. There's even another table lined with leg armor.

"Pull this stuff on," Denis says. "Take your pick. I'm going to go check on Skye."

He walks away, and I take a vest and a set of leg armor, which are basically pants made of a flexible, rubbery material with light but dense metal links laced on top of them. I pull off my shirt and pants, and then my jumpsuit underneath, and change into the new gear. The vest feels snug but comfortable, and the leg garments feel good as well. I glance across the room and see that Denis is conversing with Skye about something.

While they're doing that, I might as well take a look at some of those guns. I move over to the weapon racks, where dozens of guns are hooked onto long strips of metal that run between two poles. My eyes scan the different weapons. They land on my weapon of choice, a handheld pistol with stunning rounds as well as regular lethal bullets. I pull two electric-powered ones from the wall and place them on the two chest-height holsters on my vest.

I keep looking. I find a sniper rifle that's familiar to me, although it isn't standard issue. It's a model built for speed and accuracy, and it also has a special function built into it. Named the Headspringer among the other agents that I know, it's capable of firing six shots in under five seconds, all without reloading. And if you turn a knob on the side of the barrel, it'll change the rounds to a heavy bullet capable of ripping through eight-inch thick steel walls. I take it from the rack and strap it to my back.

And finally, I walk to the tables on the far right. Belts of grenades and smoke bombs lie on the majority of the tables, but what I'm looking for is a pair of knives. I find them and place them on each hip. Pistol, sniper rifle, knives. That should be enough for a basic mission.

I walk over to Denis and Skye, who has stood up from her desk and has a satisfied expression on her face.

"I found the other file," Skye says. "We're going to San Francisco."

EIGHTEEN

The plan is quite the opposite of simple, really. It's one where if one part goes wrong, the entire operation is going to be a failure. That's it—mistakes lead to death. And not just our death, possibly the deaths of others.

Back at Denis' hideout, Skye was able to find the location of the other file by hacking into the main system of the one we have. Part of me is surprised at how easy it was for her to do it, but I also haven't doubted her skills with computers.

San Francisco would've been one of my first guesses. Obviously, the NAIS headquarters lies directly next to the Golden Gate Bridge, and that makes the area a natural place to safeguard File 337. However, that also means that the facility is going to be swarming with security. That leads us to another major problem: Denis' communication system is down, so we have no way of contacting Thaxter or anyone else in their group. Denis chose to stay back in Hawaii at the hideout, and he'll be helping Skye, and me run the mission remotely from there.

I keep a hand on the holds above my head and walk over to the open hull doors of the bush plane we're in. Few clouds populate the blue skies around me, and I begin to see the outlines of mountains below.

Denis was able to get us this plane from an airfield close to his hideout. From there, we took it far south to avoid the blockade of NAIS battleships surrounding Hawaii. We looped back up towards the American mainland and are now somewhere near Los Angeles. We'll be in San Francisco within twenty minutes.

Unfortunately, the hard part won't be getting in or out; it'll be retrieving the file. We're currently unaware of what the NAIS is keeping the file inside of because we only have exact longitude and latitude coordinates from Skye's hack. For all we know, they could be holding it inside a peanut butter jar. My guess is that it'll be a vault of some kind, like the type they use in banks.

Denis decides that there are too many soldiers there to fight our way to the file, which means we'll be using disguises. When we get there, we'll knock out some of the guards on the Consensus' outskirts and then use the same artificial face masking device that I used in London to disguise ourselves. After that, we should be completely blended into the environment of the facility, and we'll try to get to the file.

Rather than thinking of all the ways it could go wrong, I set my mind on what would happen if everything went right for us. We'd have both files, the second one being stored in a compartment in the plane right now, and we would be able to open them and find the information that's inside. Whatever it is, it should answer so many questions for us. About the NAIS, about everything.

"We're almost there," Skye shouts from the cockpit.

Even with her raised voice, it's hard to hear over the roar of the wind outside. I make my way back to the center of the cargo hold and make sure I have all of my gear.

I feel the plane beginning to descend, and I see that the once cloudless sky has turned foggy, and I can't make out any blue. A telltale sign that we're nearing San Fransisco—the air there has thick fog covering it much of the year.

Once we get closer to the ground, I begin to see the towns that surround San Francisco. The plane turns right, and I see rolling green hills dotted with tall trees. We must be getting close to the mountains near the Consensus. On the left side of the plane, I see dawn breaking through the fog, and the sun casts beautiful rays of red, orange, and yellow across the water in the bay. Waves crash onto the shore and I see boats beginning to head out onto the bay from the pier. And then I see one of California's most famous landmarks, the Golden Gate Bridge. I've seen it before when visiting the city, but never during sunrise. The ever-growing bright light shines onto the fading red steel of the bridge's arches and casts the entire structure in a beautiful glow.

I wish I had more time to focus on our surroundings instead of always being forced to rush into these dangerous missions. All of these places we've gone to—Hawaii, London, Tokyo to name a few—they're all beautiful locations that many people around the world get to appreciate every day.

Those are the people we protect, though. If it weren't for people like Skye and me, they wouldn't be safe. We had to betray our agency because we knew it was corrupt. How many other people are there in the world like us and Denis and Thaxter and their group? I have to remind myself that this is for the right cause because if I don't, everything seems hopeless. We fight to protect the innocent people, the normal people. That does feel right.

I glance outside of the cargo hold and realize that I can't see the wings of the plane draping over the sides of the hull anymore. In the place of the massive wings, all I see is a faint blue sheen that ripples outwards where the wings are supposed to be. It takes me a quick moment before I realize that Skye must've activated the cloaking mode on this plane. I remember studying this particular type of plane back in NAIS training. It has the ability to completely cloak itself using mirrored cameras, and it can also bypass radio waves using special radar equipment that's hooked up to the hull.

I cross to the other end of the cargo hold. I can see the ground quickly drawing nearer, the tops of redwood trees nearly touching the invisible bottom of the plane. Skye continues to skim the forest until she finds a clearing that's large enough to fit the entirety of the plane. The propellers begin to slow, and the whirring noise of the landing gear touches my ears as the plane sets down.

Skye walks out from the cockpit's archway and nods to the two motorcycles lying in the cargo hold behind us.

"I landed the plane around ten miles from the Consensus grounds," she tells me. "We can take these to the base of the mountain and then begin laying the wire."

I nod in assent. "Is Denis on the comms system yet?" I ask.

She shakes her head. "My guess is that the connection here isn't good enough for him to radio us. Hopefully, we'll be able to get a signal when we get closer to the facility."

I walk to the side of the plane and push a button on a panel. The side doors of the cargo hold close, and the ramp leading up to the hold lowers. I cross to one of the motorcycles and swing my leg over it and sit on the cushion. I start the engine with the flick of a switch and drive down the ramp.

When I'm on the ground of the clearing we're in, I tap my watch and the plane's ramp folds up through the automated connection. I also press a button on it that says SENTRY, and I listen as flaps of metal fold out from the plane's exterior and shield any openings. The engines, cockpits, and windows on the plane become completely covered and my guess is that it would take more than a bomb to break through the protective armor of the plane now. Not that anyone is going to be able to see the invisible plane.

Skye and I take a path through the woods that leads to the mountains that the Consensus lies atop. When we've driven for several miles, the ground begins to slant upwards, and we stop the bikes. I cut the engine on mine and step onto the ground. The trees become less sparse as the forest floor leads to more rocky terrain. This is where we need to be more careful of the NAIS security.

I see dozens of different paths that lead up the beginning of the hill. I think that the area we're in right now is an open public space, but as we near the very top of the mountain, the zone becomes restricted.

I follow Skye up one of the paths. The ground isn't too steep right now, which makes sense given that this is a tourist park until further up. I take a glance up to the peak of the mountain and I see the gray outline of a building. My eyes scan the slope for any cameras, but we're clear for now.

As we work our way up the mountain I become increasingly weary of the buildings ahead of us. The path we're on seems to be going mostly straight. From time to time I glance at our surroundings to make sure that we're alone. It's still early in the morning, just after dawn. My guess is that the park isn't officially open yet and that rangers and tourists won't arrive for a while yet. In addition to that, I haven't spotted any NAIS guards. They must all be at the top near the facility.

After what seems like forever, the ground eventually begins to flatten out and I realize that it's because we're at the end of the tourist zone. A long gate made of dark gray metal stretches the length of the mountain and creates an intimidating structure that marks the beginning of the Consensus.

I realize that we're going to have to make our way through that gate in order to reach the facility housing the file. That'll trigger the alarm, and we'll be trapped by the rest of their forces. We're going to have to find a quick way to get down from the next mountain, which of course, is where the facility itself is.

"How do we get past that gate?" Skye asks me. We both stay crouched below the top of the ridge, and I make sure to keep my chest pressed tightly onto the ground to keep the soldiers ahead from seeing the sniper rifle that's slung across my back.

I think about it. "There aren't any other entrances to the Consensus other than this front side," I tell her. "I think that if we were able to lure two of the guards out with a distraction, then we'd be able to knock them out and use the disguise device. Hopefully, whoever we bring out is someone who has access to the main facility."

"But if not, what do we do?" she asks.

"We'll cross that bridge when we get to it," I reply. "For now, we need to just hope that we get lucky. I know it doesn't really sound like a plan, but we need to get ahold of that file soon."

She nods in return. "You make a distraction," Skye tells me. "I'll silence my guns and fire at them from the side. If we draw out at least two of them, we should be able to use the disguise device."

She gestures to the metal device hanging from her hip, the same one I utilized in London to get into Laurings' meeting.

"Sounds like a plan," I reply. "But we're going to have to come up with some excuse for why we left the gate in the first place, or rather why the guards left."

"We'll just tell them that a couple of tourists came up and we had to send them back."

I nod. "Let's do it, then."

Skye stays in her crouched position and moves thirty feet to the left, keeping her head below the ridge to stay out of sight of the guards at the gate. When she's in position, I move several yards down the hill. I pull my gun from its holster and slam the butt of it hard into a slim-looking tree. The collision rocks the trunk of the skinny pine, leaves rattle on the branches, and fall to the ground. I do it once more, this time harder. More leaves fall from the branches.

The goal of that was to make it seem like someone was pushing the tree. Luckily for me, the idea seems to work out alright. I hear voices from up ahead and the sound of the metal gate opening. Footsteps trudge across the dirt ahead of me, and I wait in silence as they grow louder. When the shadow of two guards stretches over the ridge, I duck down behind the tree, keeping out of sight. I hear two muted gunshots. The two guards crumble and drop dead on the rocky path in front of me.

Skye steps out from behind the tree she was using as cover. She blows away the small trail of smoke coming from the silencer on her gun. We both approach the guards quietly but quickly. We have to make this transformation fast in order to not draw the attention of the guards back at the gate.

I pull the face masking device from my belt and push it against the male guard's face. Three metal hooks spin out from the circular head of the device, and the pincers on the end of the hooks latch onto the guard's forehead and cheeks. I look away as I hear a low whirring noise from the device. Within ten seconds the noise stops and the hooks retract from the guard's face. A compartment on the device opens, and a metal panel extends outwards. On the panel lies a silky mask made of silicone that makes me want to feel sick. I take it off and pull it onto my face tightly. It slides on smoothly, and when I look at the shiny reflective surface of the device, I can't recognize my face.

We undergo the same process on the other guard, who is luckily female. As Skye's mask is working, I pull the male guard's thin overalls over my jumpsuit. I pull the sleeves all the way on to hide my transforming watch. In the length of a minute, we both look unrecognizable.

But the problem is my weapons. We need the sniper rifle that I'm carrying for our escape. The plan is to shoot a coil of wire out of the sniper in order to create a roughly usable zip line. We even have collapsible carabiners hooked along our belts, though they're now hidden by the guard's overalls. I need to find a way to bring the sniper with us without the other guards noticing.

"Thinking about how to smuggle the sniper in?" Skye asks me with an arched eyebrow.

She clearly noticed my thoughts.

"You know me too well," I reply. "I think I have an idea, but it'll take too long to explain out loud. Just roll with me, and we'll be fine."

Her eyebrow doesn't go down, but she nods. The two of us have a relationship built on trust, and if I say that I have a plan, she won't argue. Though I am beginning to doubt this plan myself.

Skye follows me as I head up the path. When we reach the top of the ridge, I don't think twice about what we're about to do. Obtaining the file will be worth all of this. It has to be.

The gate comes into sight again as we round the top of the hill. The twenty meters between the edge of the ridge and the gate close quickly, and before I know it, I'm standing in front of a boxy gray guardhouse flanked on either side by the imposing steel bars of the gate itself.

A guard emerges from the front metal door of the guardhouse. He looks at me with a questioning look.

"Cooper, what was over the hill?" he asks, nodding at the sniper rifle that I'm carrying in my arms.

So my name's Cooper.

"There was an old man hunting some birds. I guess he didn't realize that this was a restricted area." I motion to the sniper rifle. "I'm not sure how he got a hold of this gun, though. It's a highly advanced model."

"It is," the guard says. He narrows his eyes at the gun. "You should take it up to the Consensus headquarters for inspection. I'll let them know that you're coming. Is the man that was hunting still down there?"

I shake my head at him. "No, he ran as soon as he saw us. Stumbled and dropped this," I say, nodding again at the sniper rifle in my hands.

I think about adding 'no need to check down there', but that might seem suspicious. The only thing I need to be concentrating on right now is finding the file.

"Thanks for the help," I add. "We'll be back down here in half an hour."

The guard steps aside and opens a sliding door that leads to the other side of the guardhouse. Here a tiled pathway snakes forward towards the massive cliff face ahead of us. As we draw nearer, I spot a giant metal tower that's nestled into the side of the mountain. It must be an elevator that'll take us up to the main building of the Consensus.

We reach the elevator within thirty seconds. I place Cooper's keycard on a scanner, and it flashes green. The doors glide open, and we step inside the metal car. It's fully encased in metal walls, blocking any view of the hills surrounding us. I don't look up but can sense the presence of a video camera and an audio recording system. As the elevator begins to rise upwards, I keep my mouth shut and my hands at my side.

The doors slide open, and we emerge into a hallway. Guards stand on either side of the entrance and nod at us.

"Cooper, you're taking that rifle up to headquarters for inspection, right?" one of them asks.

I nod at him. "We'll be back here in a couple minutes," I reply.

Without further conversation, Skye and I continue down the hallway. I see her periodically glancing at her watch, checking the coordinates of the file. I follow her through a pair of double doors and onto a walkway that extends between two buildings. She squints at her watch and brings us into the building. Skye takes a right and pulls open the door to a storage room. I glance around at the dumb-down room. What's special about this?

She sees my expression and nods. "August, the file's coordinates aren't the same anymore. It's moving as we speak."

NINETEEN

"**I**t's moving?" I ask Skye, my heartbeat suddenly kicking into overdrive. "How can you be sure?"

She gestures for me to come to her. I cross the short length of the storage room and narrow my eyes at the small screen of her watch. On the glass panel is the same display of longitude and latitude coordinates we've been using to track the file's location this entire time. However, the numbers are now constantly changing in small increments. Skye is right. The file is not in the same place that it was several minutes ago.

"We have to follow it."

Skye nods. "It's possible that they're moving it to a different location. Maybe it's only been at this base for several days, and the NAIS is taking the file to the more secure locations in the city. It makes complete sense."

"You're probably right," I reply, thinking for a moment. "They must be transferring it in some type of convoy. We have to intercept it before they make it to the city. If they manage to lock it up in another vault, there's no way for us to get to it before the Shadow Group makes a move."

Skye pulls the door open and pokes her head out. When she sees that no one's there, she nods, and we step out. She continues glancing at her watch as we head down the hallway. After a few seconds, she sees something on her watch and breaks into a run. I match her pace.

"What's happening?"

Adrenaline rushes through my veins as our footsteps echo against the smooth metal floor.

Her eyes stay focused on her watch. "The coordinates are changing at a more rapid rate. If we don't get sight of the convoy now, we'll lose it for sure."

The hallway ends at another metal door. I push it open, and we emerge onto a long glass walkway that spans across a slight gorge between two buildings. My eyes follow Skye's gaze as she looks northwest, and I realize what she's seeing. There's a long winding road leading down from the Consensus on this side of the mountain, and a long convoy of armored black cars is making their way out of the area. They must have the file.

Skye points a finger further down the road. "They're heading for the bridge."

She's right. The mountainous road opens up onto a much larger freeway that's bustling with cars. Not more than a tenth of a mile of that freeway stretches before reaching the massive red iron structure of the Golden Gate Bridge.

"We can catch the convoy on the bridge," I say, my mind working rapidly as I formulate a plan.

I unsling my sniper rifle from my back, and Skye's reaction is instantly one of bewilderment.

"August, there's no way that's going to work," she says cautiously. "We have a better chance of finding transportation and catching up to the convoy than with what you want to do."

I wink at her. "Sorry, my mind's already set on it." I grin at her. "Besides, if we've come this far, anything's possible."

"Fine, but we have to do it extremely quickly and precisely."

I look into her deep blue eyes. "Wouldn't have it any other way."

She chuckles. "Let's do this."

I study the distance between us and the famous steel bridge. It's no farther than six hundred yards from where I stand, though the ground slopes downward significantly because of the hill. I glance down both sides of the walkway. We're by ourselves. What I have in mind is both the most rewarding way for us to intercept the convoy and the most dangerous.

I pull a coiled rope from my belt. It's a thin metal Kevlar wire that's easily looped around itself for over a mile. I open a small hatch on my sniper rifle and feed it through. This model is a state-of-the-art weapon, but that's not the only thing that it can be used for.

I feed the wire into the opening in the rifle, and when several inches of it are inside, a motor activates. It pulls the wire in quickly, and the thin metal rope unravels in my hands. Within twenty seconds, the entirety of the Kevlar wire is inside my sniper rifle.

I walk to the railing and set the sniper onto it, pulling two legs out from either side of it. It locks itself onto the metal rail, and I put my eye to the scope. I maneuver the sniper's scope toward the bridge. On the freeway, in front of the bridge, the convoy has caused the traffic flow to stop. Cars back away from the oncoming line of massive black vehicles. I turn the scope towards the bridge itself. I have to find a strong connection point for the wire to latch onto.

My eye lands on a junction between the rising arch of the bridge's diagonal beams and a wide iron crossbar that runs across the center of the bridge. I line up the shot perfectly, accounting for the slight wind coming at me. I take three breaths as I always do before firing a scoped shot. My finger wraps around the trigger. I pull it.

The harpoon-like metal tip flies out towards the bridge, taking the silvery metal wire with it. I stand back up and put my eye to the scope. A good ten seconds pass until the sound of the wire uncoiling inside the rifle stops.

I allow myself a brief grin. It was an utterly perfect shot. Everything about it—the timing, the arc, the account for a slight breeze—was perfect. I see the tip of the coil embedded into the exact junction I was aiming for. It'll hold itself steady when we head across.

The convoy's reached the front of the bridge. I nod at Skye, and we both reach to our belts. I find two carabiners and a small metal bar all connected together to form a trolley-like machine. This is far from a tourist zip line adventure, but we'll make do with the equipment we have.

"You want to go first?" I ask Skye, who's still getting her carabiners ready.

She shakes her head. "You go first, and I'll get on right after you. If we unlatch ourselves from the line right as we reach the front cars, it's possible for us to take the convoy. And we have a better chance if we're together."

"See you on the other side."

I swing my right leg over the railing, then my left. I sit carefully on the metal railing and clip the two carabiners onto the line. They'll hang in front of me, and the metal bar will give me something to hold on to, acting like a guide.

I keep my feet on the railing for a second more, and then I kick off. I feel my legs hanging in the air, and I grip the bar in front of me as tight as I can. The wind rushes around me and whips my hair. The iconic red steel bridge's looming presence becomes larger and larger by the second. I hear cars passing under me, and I realize that the convoy is passing directly under me too. I'm moving slightly faster than it.

The sound of my carabiners scraping against the metal wire intensifies. I'm speeding up rapidly. The junction where I shot the tip of this wire comes into sight barely thirty meters away. The first several cars at the head of the convoy are directly underneath me. I decide to go for the second one.

I reach to my holster for my gun. I pull It out and aim it at the hook that's holding the carabiners to my belt. I fire.

Sparks fly from the metal, and the hooks fly apart. As the carabiners come off of the line, I feel my fingers graze the wire above. The tiny barbs of metal scrape into my skin, but I don't have time to cry out in pain before I'm released from the wire and fall. Everything seems to freeze and rush by, all at the same moment. I have no control as I fall straight down toward the convoy.

My knees buckle as my feet slam into the roof of a black sedan. I gasp as I feel tendrils of pain shoot all the way up to my hips. I fell ten feet while moving at forty miles an hour. I was too distracted by the pain coming from my hands that I forgot to brace for the impact.

I hear voices coming from the car below. I hear one of the windows rolling down beneath me, and a soldier pokes his head out, looking up at the roof. I turn a knob on my pistol, and it turns to non-lethal rounds. I fire it directly at the soldier's forehead.

He shouts out in pain and falls back inside. I hear the cock of a gun, and I roll to the side just in time as a round of bullets pounds upwards through the roof of the car. I catch myself just as I'm about to fall off the edge of the car, the blood from my fingers staining the matte black of the roof.

I grunt, my feet still aching from the impact. I lean over the edge and fire several shots at the car's front wheels. It punctures the tire, and the elastic material deflates. I watch another sedan pass by next to me, and I make a leaping jump onto its roof. Several yards to my left, the other car flips over on itself and slams into the side of the bridge. The debris catches another car that's part of the convoy and forces it to stop. Two birds with one stone.

I hear the sound of carabiners scraping against wire, and I realize that

Skye is here as well. I look up from my place atop the roof of the moving sedan and see Skye unclip herself from the line. She falls downward, and it all happens so much quicker than it felt when I fell. Skye lands gracefully atop a car behind me.

I tap my ear with one hand while keeping the other firmly planted on the ski-like hold that lines either side of the sedan. My earbud and mic activate.

"Where is the file's signal right now?" I shout into the mic over the wind.

"It's centered inside that massive truck," Skye replies.

I look back at the convoy from my place atop the moving car. Two more black sedans trail the ones that Skye and I are holding onto. After the two of them, I spot a massive military truck that's carrying a rectangular black trailer that's over twenty meters long. I can see armored plating running across the front of the truck and through the box. I'm not sure I've ever seen a military vehicle meant for land transport larger than this one.

"We need to get aboard that truck." I look at the car below me. They haven't noticed that I'm on top of them yet. "I'm going to try to slow down the car I'm on to let the truck catch up to me. I'll find a way to get on top of it."

Static crackles. "Alright," she replies. "I'll figure out something. See you on that truck."

As our conversation ends, I pull a knife from my belt. Keeping one hand securely on the roof-holds of the car, I lean down over the right side of the sedan. My eyes search for the rim of the rear right tire, and I find it. I jab the knife deep inside the rubber of the wheel that's closest to the top of the rim. The material deflates instantly as it did before, and I feel the weight of the car tip to the right. Sparks fly from the metal undercarriage of the car, scraping against the concrete road. I feel the rest of the car trying to pull forward, but the broken tire slows it down immensely.

Bullets pop out of the roof of the car, and I roll to the side, my legs dangling in open air. The soldiers in there have finally realized I'm up here. I take my own firearm and return fire, aiming exactly where I know the soldiers will be seated. My advantage is my knowledge of the soldiers' positions; they're firing blindly. Within two seconds, the return fire from the two rear passenger seats has ceased completely.

I realize that the truck has completely caught up to us. Its engine roars, and the box it's carrying seems even larger than before. If I had to guess, I'd estimate there are at least a dozen guards in there.

"I'm on the truck," Skye says. "Where are you?"

I grin, wondering how she'd gotten on there before me. "One second," I reply. "Working on it."

As the back of the truck takes over the rapidly slowing sedan, I wait for a good spot to jump to. Most of the boxy shape is completely flat, but I see a curved metal ladder at the back. When the truck is about to completely overtake the sedan, I jump off of the car and into the five-foot void. My hands land on the bars, but my vertical leap wasn't strong enough. My knees slam into the concrete below me, and the truck's speed causes my legs to be dragged roughly across the road. I scream in pain, and I kick my feet against the concrete, trying to push myself up. I get a better hold of the ladder and pull myself up, using all of the core strength that I have. When my legs are clear of the concrete, I see a hand reaching down, and I'm glad it's Skye's. I take her hand, and she helps me up the ladder.

I pause for a brief moment on the roof of the truck. Searing pain is coming from my knees, and when I look at them, I almost collapse. The skin is completely torn apart, red gashes running across both legs. Skye kneels next to me.

"Can you stand?" she asks.

I nod, pushing myself up. "I think I'll be fine."

I hear a whirring noise, and my attention goes to the center of the truck's load. Three armed soldiers step out of an opening in the flat roof. I'm about to roll to the side to avoid their fire when I hear an explosion come from behind them. A massive cloud of smoke erupts, and when it clears, two of the soldiers are missing, and I can see the charred and mutilated body of the third. I glance at Skye.

"Was that you?" I ask, knowing that it was.

"Guilty as charged," she replies. "And before you talk about not killing, this mission is too important to be stopping for things like that. These soldiers probably know what Taylor's up to, and they're still working for her. There's no reason to spare the lives of people that have already lost their own purpose."

I nod solemnly. This is the Skye that I remember—the no-shit, always on top of things, Skye. I realize that this is what I missed about when we were mission partners. That thought leads to me knowing that I love her, even if she doesn't know it. I'm going to have to tell her soon.

Skye walks across the moving roof to the opening. It's a large circular hole in the roof, and she pokes her head inside and immediately comes back out. I hear bullets ricocheting off of metal walls. There's still a lot of firepower inside.

"Any ideas?" Skye asks, keeping her eyes trained on the opening.

"Yeah, I actually have one," I reply.

I pull two small round objects from my belt, each one with a pin on top. Skye sees them and understands what I'm thinking, but she still has a questioning look on her face.

"How will we see through the smoke?" she asks.

"You won't need to," I tell her. "Just don't punch me, and we'll be fine."

She rolls her eyes. "August, we'll be gunned down as soon as we step through that hole."

I shake my head and gesture to a third round device that I've pulled from my belt. It's a newly developed EMP-like device that'll render nearby weapons useless for over a minute. A smile spreads across Skye's face at the sight of it.

"I like our odds," I tell her. "Let's get that file."

I walk to the opening and pull the pin on the smoke grenade first. I count two seconds and then throw it inside the truck. I hear a small explosion, and gray gas begins to leak out of the opening. The smoke that the device emits is strong and will last longer than we need.

As coughs start to come from the soldiers inside the truck, I twist a knob on the EMP. I hear a hum come from it, followed by the sound of clicks coming from both Skye's and my weapons and the soldiers'. In a matter of a second, guns within fifty meters of us are now useless. I keep a mental note that we have two minutes before weapons are viable again.

Skye drops down through the opening hatch first, and I follow her quickly. I land softly on a metal floor, my knees burning a little bit from the drop. I follow Skye to the left, where the smoke is the least dense. The soldiers may not be able to see anything, but we can't either. Tactile senses and my ears are the tools I have to work with.

Skye knows this as well, and the sound of her footsteps is completely imperceptible, like mine. However, the soldiers are in shock from the smoke and then the EMP. Their footsteps are loud and echoing.

I hear a soldier cry out as Skye strikes them. I dash to the far right, moving around the hazy outline of a chair. I sense movement ahead of me, and when the rough outline of an NAIS soldier comes into view, I send my foot slamming into their chest. They fall backward, and I follow the attack through with a sharp hit to the stomach. The soldier crashes backward, and the sound of glass breaking follows.

I can still hear more loud footsteps ahead. I've kept track of how far we've gone through the truck, and I think that we're halfway down to the back. Also, another minute on the EMP's effects.

I hear Skye cry out ahead of me, and my gait turns into a sprint. I see her lying on the ground, a soldier standing over her with a knife. I kick off against the wall and land on the soldier, my knee slamming into his neck. I knock him to the ground, and his head slams against metal. Blood trickles from his head, and I know that I've broken his neck.

A soldier tackles me to the ground and my back slams against metal pipes that run across the floor. I shout in pain, and the breath is knocked out of me as the soldier follows through with a punch to my upper chest. I gather what little strength I have left and dodge his next blow. I roll to the side of him and nimbly push myself to my feet.

The soldier rushes at me, using his shoulder and arm like a ram. I sidestep him and jump high into the air, swinging my leg out at him. My boot catches him in the cheek, and he falls to the ground. I snake towards him, my muscles burning from the physical exertion. I wind my arm up and swing my fist at the soldier's face as hard as I can. He falls unconscious.

My mental count of the EMP hits me, and I hear the click of guns coming back online. I heard four in total: Mine and Skye's, but also two more. There are still at least two soldiers left on this truck.

I hear voices coming from behind me, and the smoke begins to clear. I raise my gun in the direction of the voices and am dismayed to see two soldiers holding Skye at gunpoint. She's shaking a little bit, and I see a knife embedded deep into her left thigh.

"Drop your gun," one of them shouts at me.

They press the barrel of their gun harder into Skye's temple. My heart sinks at the movement.

Before I can think about what I'm about to do, I turn my gun and fire at the ceiling above the soldiers. The bullets puncture a set of metal pipes that must filter the air in here. The massive pipes fall downward, and the soldiers release Skye at the sight. I run forward and grab Skye's arm just in time to pull her away from the falling pipes. One of the pipes hits a soldier hard in the head, and when the echoing of the pipes hitting the floor has ended, I spot the remaining soldier running down the truck toward the front. I raise my gun and end her life in a single shot.

I kneel on the cold metal floor next to Skye, keeping my eye trained on the front of the truck, where the massive box is connected to the driver and passenger seats of the truck itself. Skye's breaths come quick, and I realize that the knife wound is even worse than I thought. The knife is deep in her thigh, almost halfway to the hilt of the knife. Pools of blood run across the ground around her.

"I'm going to have to take it out," I tell her.

I offer her my hand, and she takes it and holds it tightly.

"Ready?" I ask.

She nods. I pull it out in one quick, fluid motion. She gasps and screams in pain. I throw the knife to the side and place her hand on the wound. "Keep pressure on that."

I stand and look through the truck for a first aid kit. I see one strapped to the wall next to a set of computer monitors. I run to it and pull it off. When I return to Skye, I see that she's kept the wound under pressure, and the bleeding has mostly stopped. I open the first aid kit and pull a bandage out. I unwrap it and tie it around her leg, making sure that the wound is completely covered. The cloth instantly becomes completely soaked in scarlet.

I take a tube of cream from the first aid kit. It's a specialized medicine that'll freeze the wound for a short time. I squeeze the glaze onto the bandage, and a blue sheen spreads across it. Skye sighs in relief, and I know that the pain must've alleviated slightly.

"August," Skye rasps. "Help me up."

I nod and help pull her to her feet. She puts her arm around my shoulder and then points her finger at the back of the truck.

"The file?" I ask.

"Yeah," she says shakily. "It's coming from that cabinet."

I help Skye limp to the back of the truck. There's a massive iron cabinet built into the wall. There's a fingerprint scanner on it, and I realize that there's no way we can break through the four-inch thick metal. Our only option is opening it properly.

I look through the truck at the dead soldiers. None of their biometrics will work now that they're dead. I don't know what to do.

It strikes me that the last time we tried to open a safe that was holding one of the twin files, my fingerprint had worked. I can't even hope that the same thing will happen this time, but we have no other options.

I press my thumb to the scanner, and nothing happens. Skye and I wait in frozen silence, both of us unsure what to do. We wait for longer than a minute, neither of us moving.

Skye shakes her head and steps up to the scanner. I'm confused about what she's about to do. She presses her own thumb to the scanner, and for a moment, nothing happens. But after several seconds, a lock clicks, and the doors of the cabinet hiss open. Mist flows out of the cabinet, and when it clears, I see the file suspended in midair, held up by the same three metal wires we saw back in Hawaii. The file is completely identical to its twin other than the number engraved on it: 337. A small breath escapes me, and I realize that this is the end of a long journey.

Skye gasps as well, and we both laugh.

"My dad left me clearance," Skye whispers. "I'll have to ask him about this later. We did it."

I'd forgotten that Skye is the daughter of Luke Wren, the director of the NAIS. I slowly nod, reaching into a compartment in my jumpsuit. I pull out a small metal case with a much smaller thumb scanner on it. I place my thumb on it, and it clicks open, revealing the other file lying on a bed of silver velvet cloth. Skye takes the file from the cabinet, and we hold the two files next to each other, a perfect match.

I realize that Skye is staring into my eyes, not at the files. I find myself looking back at her, and in that moment, as I stare at her beautiful green eyes, I know that I have to do it.

"Skye," I say, my voice barely a whisper. "I can't imagine any person I would rather be with right now."

She leans towards me, and I hold her face in my hands. She does the same. We are locked together in this one moment, and it seems to last forever. The words come from me first.

"I love you, Skye," I tell her.

She chuckles. "I love you, too."

And then we close the gap, and my lips are pressing against hers. She kisses me back, and joy flows through my body. Her touch feels so right. We hold each for a minute, our lips locked together. This is what love feels like. And I'm sharing it with the most important person in my world.

TWENTY

After a long time, we pull apart from each other. Both of us laugh a little bit at the rush of it all.

"I've wanted to do that for so long," she says.

"Me too," I reply. "I wish we could just stay here forever, together."

"I know," Skye says, still staring into my eyes. "But we've got to go. Kissing is great, but we've gotta save the world."

I chuckle at that. "We should make a move towards the front of the truck."

"I agree," she says. "But first, what do we do with these files?"

She hands me File 337, and I hold the twin files together. I'm not sure why, but I feel stronger holding the two of them, like part of me is more complete. It must be because of the journey it took to get to this point.

I notice two small nooks on the first file. Where the nooks are present on the first, two nodes jut out of the second. I push them together, and I find that they fit perfectly. I expect something to happen, for a hologram to pop up or a message to ring out. But nothing comes.

"Look," Skye says, squinting at the files in my hands.

I follow her line of sight. A line of text has appeared on the small front screen of the file. It reads SIGNAL UNABLE TO BE BROADCASTED.

"What does that mean?" I ask, knowing that she'll likely know. Computer genius and all.

She thinks about it for a moment. "I think that the data on these files is too large to be broadcasted from the files themselves. My guess is that we're going to need a much larger booster array to be able to read what's on here."

"Where's the nearest satellite broadcaster from here?" I say.

She looks into my eyes again. "The only place I know has a satellite with enough power to read the signal is the NAIS Headquarters."

"We're going to have to get there, then," I tell her. "We don't have any other choice, really. This truck is already heading there."

"Alright," she replies. "But even if we took the convoy over and reached the satellite, how could we possibly hope to hold off the entire NAIS force at the headquarters? We don't have any backup. Denis has been a complete no-show."

"Only up to this point, young lady," Denis says over the radio. I didn't realize he joined the comms system. "I've got a plan for you two to get those files open."

"Nice to hear your voice," Skye says. "What do you have in mind?"

"I got a hold of Thaxter," Denis replies. "Turns out he didn't blow up when the plane went out. He's been regrouping with some of his contacts. Only reason he didn't show up was because he found out that his comms had been compromised by someone. Still unsure who that is. Any-who, Thaxter's assembled a force of roughly fifty soldiers. All highly-trained and elite at what they do. I'm going to be directing them along with you two to get you inside the NAIS compound safely. They'll hold off the NAIS until you're able to get ahold of what's inside the files."

"That's a very detailed plan you've got going," I say. "Keep us updated, okay?"

"Affirmative," he says. "I'll tell you more as you near the city."

Skye and I exchange a glance. "I think we need to take the truck now," I say.

She nods. "We have to do it quietly, though, so that the rest of the convoy doesn't notice."

We head down the length of the truck and reach a wall at the end. Two massive metal doors stretch across the wall, and a plaque reads COCKPIT. I try one of the door handles, and it slides open.

Two seats lie in front of a wall of controls and levers. This truck's features are much different than a standard one. A soldier is at the wheel, and another turns around as we enter. He opens his mouth to shout, but Skye and I shoot both of the soldiers before they can do anything.

I push the driver out of his seat and onto the floor. I climb into the driver's seat and keep the truck steady. Skye closes the doors behind us and locks them before joining me.

I hadn't noticed that we'd entered the city while we were fighting the soldiers in the back of the truck. The convoy, missing several more cars than it'd started with, is making its way up a steep hill that stretches through a quiet neighborhood of quaint houses. I realize that a barricade has been set up on the street, and no other cars roam the streets around the path the convoy is taking. This file is important enough to warrant a full-on military disruption.

We continue making our way up the hill, the streets quiet and the convoy keeping together. I keep driving for over fifteen minutes before I finally catch a glimpse of the NAIS compound. It's a sprawling expanse of dozens of white square buildings, with walkways connecting them. Dozens of guards patrol the area, and I see drones hovering in the air above the complex. A massive iron gate encompasses the buildings. I notice that the streets surrounding the compound are comprised of power generation buildings and satellite dishes—nothing recreational or civilian anywhere near the NAIS headquarters.

I see one of the screens in front of me change. It displays an incoming message from the NAIS. They want us to initiate a call to the compound. I glance at Skye. We both know that if we don't speak to them, they'll become suspicious of the security of the convoy. We don't have a choice.

I reach forward and turn a knob on the dashboard in front of me. Static crackles as the radio activates. A voice comes through.

"This is Officer Kane reporting from NAIS Base 1A," a woman says. "Am I speaking to the convoy that departed from the Consensus approximately thirty-two minutes ago?"

"Affirmative," I reply, keeping my voice steady.

I glance at the driver's dead body. I see a name tag clipped onto his chest. I identify myself as the soldier.

"This is Lieutenant Jon Parol. We're approaching the complex as we speak."

There's a pause.

"We see you nearing the compound's gate," Officer Kane replies. "We heard from the other vehicles in your convoy that you may have experienced an incursion from two unidentified assailants. Can you confirm that?"

They're talking about us.

"Affirmative," I reply. "At the moment, we don't know of their whereabouts, but we can confirm that our payload is secure. Requesting permission to enter the compound?"

We've almost reached the gate. At least half a dozen armed guards are waiting at the large outpost that marks the entry point.

"First, we need your convoy's verification code. We cannot grant you entry without it. The Deputy Director is requiring a high level of precaution right now."

Taylor. That's who she's talking about. Somehow, she must have gotten footage of Skye's and my attack on the convoy. She must be panicking, realizing that two highly-trained agents that she presumed were dead weeks ago are alive.

"We'll get you that code," I reply, my panic sinking in.

How on earth are we meant to get to that satellite now?

"Over and out," I add.

Skye glances at me. "Where do we go now?"

Denis' voice comes through right on cue. It's as if every time we need help, he's there at that exact moment.

"I've been listening in on that conversation. Any second now, you'll see a large military plane coming in from the east. That's Thaxter. He's got around a hundred highly-trained soldiers that are loyal to them. Once the NAIS catches sight of them, they'll forget about your convoy for the time being. That distraction will leave you two enough time to get into the base and, hopefully, to the satellite. How you're going to do that is up to you." Static follows, and Denis' voice stops.

"Everything's got to be done ourselves, huh?" Skye asks me.

I nod. "I do have a plan to get us in, though. As soon as we see Thaxter, we're going to ram straight into that gate."

Skye's eyebrows raise. "Does this truck really have enough armor to get through that?" She asks, pointing at the imposing steel wall before us.

"Hopefully," I reply, without a drop of humor in my voice.

Skye stays silent. She's clearly tired of my wayward plans. But she also knows that they've worked so far. She's going to have to trust me if we want to get these files open.

Suddenly my eyes catch sight of a dark gray plane in the sky. Skye sees it, too, and we both stare out the windshield toward it. It becomes larger, and we realize that it's dropping its altitude steeply. I see the guards at the gate in front of us shouting to one another. Before long, an alarm begins to blare inside the compound. I hear the whir of turrets beginning to be activated.

"Now's our chance," Skye says.

I slam my foot on the accelerator, and the truck rushes forward. The guards turn towards us and raise their weapons. When we don't stop, they open fire. Their bullets ricochet off of the bulletproof glass In front of us, barely leaving a mark. They dive out of the way as we get closer. I brace as the front of the truck nears the iron gate.

The truck's massive front bumper slams into the gate, and the overwhelming mass of the truck cripples the metal gate. The gate collapses like falling dominoes as the truck crushes it and rides over the top of it. Ahead of us, NAIS soldiers are moving onto the front lawn of the compound, their weapons pointed skyward. I see soldiers parachuting out of the plane, diving down toward the ground. Dozens of Thaxter's soldiers plummet downwards, angled at the compound. Turrets send massive rounds at the plane, and soon the plane erupts in a massive explosion.

I think the entire strike force of soldiers made it off the plane. My jaw clenches as several of the NAIS soldiers' bullets hit true and riddle holes in the parachutes of Thaxter's soldiers. Those whose chutes are hit fall downwards without control, their bodies slamming hard into the ground, life instantly leaving their bodies. Others manage to deploy their chutes, and they land successfully on the roof of the compound. I search for Thaxter's face but can't find him.

Our truck has almost reached the main section of the NAIS compound. Soldiers are turning their attention to us, and I feel one of the truck's tires collapse as bullets puncture it. I slow the truck down and kick the door open. I dive outside, keeping behind the truck so that I'm not in range of the oncoming fire.

Skye crawls over to me, her pistol held in her hand. Her knife wound seems to be holding up alright for the moment.

"Do you know where the satellite dish is?" I shout over the gunfire.

"Yes," she replies. "It's near the center of the complex, located on the largest building. We won't be able to make it there, though. Access there is heavily restricted, and there are dozens of locked doors that we would have to get through to reach it."

Skye points at a smaller section of the compound. I wish I was more familiar with this base as she is.

"Over there is the power distribution center. If we can get there, I can disable all of the systems in the base that use electricity, save for the satellite dish. It'll disable the security systems long enough for us to reach the dish."

I nod. "Let's do it."

Skye guides me to the left of the truck's remaining skeleton. We work our way to the left, using the smoke of the fire around us as cover. I follow her down a walkway that winds in the direction she'd pointed out earlier. After several minutes of running, we reach the building. It's a small boxy structure supported by wide iron pillars. Skye pulls open the double metal doors at the front of it, holding her pistol out in front of her. I do the same.

We enter a short hallway that branches off in two directions. It's lit from beneath the grated floor panels by an iridescent blue light, giving the room an eerie hue.

Skye gestures to a door on the left and then makes a cross symbol with her hands, representing that there are people inside. Sure enough, I hear several muffled voices coming through the door and the clacking of keyboards. Skye edges closer to the door and places her hand on the handle, and pulls it open.

I rush forward at her side. My eyes immediately go to the three figures sitting in chairs that lie in front of a wide range of computer monitors. I fire shots at each one of them. Skye does the same, and each one of the seated figures slumps backward, dead. Skye walks forward to one of the panels in front of her. Her fingers dance across the panel, and within seconds she's finished. I feel a low hum come from around me, and I realize that it's the sound of the security systems deactivating. The display on the screens in front of me transforms from live video feeds to blank black backdrops. Skye did as she said she would. The systems are down.

"To the satellite?" I ask.

"Yeah," she replies. "We should be able to make it there without too much issue."

To my surprise, the path there is completely unobscured by any guards. My eyes flit across the grass interspersed between walkways and catch the imprints of rushed footsteps running in the direction of the front lawn. Denis must've chosen a strong group of soldiers to cause a distraction. Many of the guards here have been ordered to back up the others that are fighting.

I realize that we're almost there, almost at the dish. The twin files begin to feel heavier in my pants pocket. Within the next hour, we will know what's inside of them. What we've been in search of for all this time.

TWENTY-ONE

The satellite dish is a massive structure that spans the length of four buildings. It's supported at the base by dozens of iron lattices crisscrossed on top of each other to create a foundation. A sloped wall leads up from the base to a wide circular metal junction that holds up the dish. Like most other modern satellite dishes, the dish is reminiscent of a crater, with a wide circular circumference that slants down as it moves inward. At the center of the dish is a massive antenna, which is what's actually going to be able to download the information on the files. Four poles surround the antenna and meet in the center of the dish, creating a sharp point known as the receiving horn.

"Skye," I say, leading us across a metal walkway that connects to the satellite building. "We have to work fast. I'll hook the files up to the data cartridge, and you get the systems online. Because we shut down the security measures of the base, there shouldn't be any access problems."

"Got it," Skye replies, the echo of our boots clanging against the meshed metal floor ringing in my ears.

I hear gunshots coming from behind us. Thaxter and his team are still holding the soldiers back for now.

We climb a set of stairs that lead up to a small platform. In front of us lies the latticed base of the entire structure. I walk along the platform until I reach a wall lined with control panels, levers, and screens. I crouch and find a small glass panel, pulling it open to reveal a mess of wires inside. As I begin to plug the files into the cartridge for data extraction, Skye moves to the right and begins working on starting the dish's systems.

I find a screen that displays the text SYSTEM BLACKOUT: MANUAL OVERRIDE REQUIRED FOR LARGE DATA EXTRACTION.

"Skye, we've got a problem," I say.

She rushes over to me.

"What is it? I thought you got the files hooked up to the cartridge."

"I know," I reply. "But it won't matter."

I gesture to the screen, and her eyebrows raise when she reads the text.

"I'm going to have to go back to the compound's server room in order to do a manual reset of the dish's systems. It'll be fairly quick when I get there, but the problem will be, well, getting there," she says.

"Go. I'll have Thaxter organize a distraction. Be careful."

She nods. "I'll be back before you know I'm gone." She pulls my hand to her and holds it for a second. "I love you. This will all be over soon."

I stare back at her. "I hope it will. I love you, too."

A voice comes from behind me that chills me to the bone. One that I never imagined I'd hear again, one that I know all too well.

"Well, this is a heartfelt goodbye, isn't it?" Oscar Laurings says.

My hand goes to my holster, and as I try to pull out my gun, a bullet ricochets off the floor, just inches away from my foot.

"Drop it," Laurings tells me.

I drop the gun, and it clangs against the metal below me as I do. I look up at him, my eyes meeting his icy blue ones. I can hear Skye shifting her weight next to me. Her gun is on the ground as well. My gaze returns to Laurings. A long scar runs down his face, stretching from his temple down to his chin. I see a mixture of calm and rage in his expression that forces me to remember how well this man can get into one's head. I have to block out his words so that his thoughts don't get into mine.

"I don't want to have to hurt either of you." He points his gun at us. "You two are both very valuable to me, but nothing is more valuable than what you possess." He nods at the glass panel that conceals the files. "Bring those to me, and I will take you in—unharmed."

Neither of us replies. Laurings doesn't move, but a small smile starts to spread across his face. He gives a slight and subtle nod of his head, and I hear footsteps coming from behind him. Hunter climbs onto the platform next to Laurings, a long assault rifle in his hands. My eyes widen. His face is completely unscathed, his body protected by a sleek black suit of combat armor. Anything short of a mini-gun wouldn't penetrate that suit.

Skye trembles next to me, and I hear her whisper the words, "It can't be."

I can't speak. I saw Hunter die with my own eyes, saw my bullet penetrate his chest, and his body tumble backward over a cliff. I saw Laurings' battleship sink deep into the Pacific Ocean in an image of fire and destruction. How can it be that these two killers are still alive?

Skye makes a clicking noise with her tongue. I instantly recognize her signal. I whip my arm out in front of me and activate my shield. Laurings' lips curve into a grin, and he raises his gun and fires at me. I run sideways toward the edge of the platform, bullets clanging against the metal of my shield. When I reach the edge, I jump high over the metal railing. As my eyes turn towards what's below the platform, I realize that it's a twenty-foot fall downwards. My mind races as the air rushes around me.

I raise my shield to my shoulder as I brace for the impact. The polished round dome of the shield slams hard Into the concrete, and my body crashes hard into the stone. I cry out in pain and try to push myself to my feet. My limbs feel shaky. Some of my bones feel broken, but I'm not sure if they are. My eyes survey the shadowed area around me for Skye.

She's locked in a choke-hold with Hunter, the two of them around twenty feet away from me on the ground. I try to force myself to my feet, but as I do, I stumble and crash to rough pavement. I watch through hazy vision as Skye throws a punch at Hunter and forces him away. Hunter collapses backward and limps away. Normally the blow that Skye struck Hunter with would've knocked him out, but he has that nearly impenetrable suit on.

My hand goes to my belt, and I find a small bottle filled with pills. Strong painkillers meant for situations like these, where my body is hurt badly, and I need to catch my breath. I pop three of them in my mouth, and my muscles begin to loosen. After half a minute, I force myself to my feet and half-walk, half-stumble over to Skye.

When I reach her, Hunter is nowhere to be seen. I notice a small trail of scarlet leading away from Skye, and it branches off towards one of the nearby buildings. I make sure to keep alert.

I kneel next to her. She's lying on her back, breaths coming rapidly. Her shield isn't deployed like mine, and I realize that her arm is dislocated. My guess is that she and Hunter got locked onto each other, and they both took the fall together. Skye's suit is strong enough to have kept her from breaking major bones, so my guess is that Hunter hit the ground and broke the fall for her.

I look back up towards the platform, searching for any sign of Laurings or Hunter. Neither is anywhere to be seen.

"Alright," I tell Skye, placing my hand on her arm. "This is going to hurt."

Skye grits her teeth. I snap her arm backward, moving it sharply back into the socket. She shouts out in pain, and it makes me flinch. When I'm sure that her arm is back in place, I help her stand up. Other than her arm, she seems to be fine, though flecks of blood dot her forehead.

She motions for me to follow her, and she leads us under the overhang of one of the buildings. Both of us keep our guard up, my gun raised, Skye in a defensive stance. She must've lost her pistol.

"August," Skye says shakily.

She reaches into her pocket and pulls out the two small chips that I know all too much about. My eyebrows raise.

"How do you have those?" I ask her.

"Laurings was distracted by you running across the platform with your shield, and Hunter must not have a firearm. As he was trying to get to me, I got to the data chamber and removed the two files. That's when he tackled me."

I nod, the event making more sense to me. Still, Skye continues to amaze me.

"What are we going to do now?" she asks.

"You head to the server room and initiate the manual reset," I tell her. "I'll make my way back up to the platform. I'd bet my life that he's up there still. He'll be waiting for me to return. I swear to god I'm going to kill him." I feel determination in my voice. We lock eyes.

"Be careful, and come back to me," I say.

Skye nods. "I will."

I lean towards her, and she leans into me. Our lips press against each other, and I let my worries wash away for a moment as the world fades to just me and her. We stay unmoving for several moments before we each finally take a step back. Both of us chuckle.

It seems oddly fitting that Skye and I are falling in love with all that's going on in the world right now. Her kiss still lingering on my lips, I turn away and begin running toward the satellite dish. I don't dare to look back —I don't dare to believe that that was the last time I'll ever see her—that that was the last kiss we'll ever share.

TWENTY-TWO

can't ignore the empty pit in my stomach that I feel at the thought of facing Laurings. I told Skye that I'd kill Laurings, but the truth is that Laurings still terrifies me even after coming face-to-face with him several times in the past. He is still the same stone-hearted, merciless killer that could send me to my own grave if I'm not careful.

The silhouette of the satellite is prominent above me, the giant parabolic dish swathing the ground in shadows. Keeping my back to the wall, I make my way up the side of a twisting ramp that will bring me up the backside of the dish's platform, the opposite direction that I came from before. Laurings is likely waiting for me at the top, guessing at my moves before I've decided to make them. Still, entering the platform on the walkway would be suicide. Even if Laurings is expecting me to come from this side, at least there are overhangs and pipes that provide some cover along the way up.

Once I near the top of the winding ramp, I take my gun from its holster and realize that the EMP device I used earlier in the convoy is recharged. The device was designed to recoup its energy over time, and it's been over an hour since I last used it. I pull the round black object from my belt and twist the knob on the side of it. A click sounds from my gun, and I hear a resounding one come from overhead, confirming that Laurings is there and that his gun is rendered useless.

I climb the rest of the way up the ramp with the knowledge that Laurings is unarmed. As I reach the platform, I immediately lock eyes with him. He's standing around twenty yards away, dead center in the middle of the platform. His eyes are narrowed with an intense malice that makes me want to tear my gaze away. But I keep my eyes trained on his piercing blue ones.

Laurings pulls his gun from his holster, and for a moment, I think that the EMP didn't work on his weapon. After a second, he drops the gun on the platform floor, and it makes a resounding clang that echoes across the open space.

I don't understand the meaning of the move, but I do feel a sense of relief to know that I'll be fighting Laurings in hand-to-hand combat. I have no doubt that he's physically stronger than me, but I do know that I'm lighter and faster on my feet. This is an opponent that will use his cunning to get the better of me. I have to use the sparse advantages that I can find.

Laurings and I circle each other on the platform, both of us making soft and careful steps. He pretends to dart forward, and I fall for it, taking a rapid step backward.

My breaths come faster and faster, and I have to force myself to slow them down. I keep my eyes trained on Laurings and feel as though I can see right through him. This man slaughters innocent people just because he can. He's a trained killer, an assassin, a terrorist, even. He has murdered thousands, and he poses a threat to the security of not only our nation but the entire world. The information contained in the twin files, whatever it is, is too valuable to fall into the hands of this man. And I won't let it.

As I stare into his deep eyes, I know why I'm going to kill him.

He has taken many things from me, so many things from this nation. He's helped corrupt the NAIS and killed countless soldiers in pursuit of information that is too precious for his eyes. And he took Hunter from me, the boy that I knew since I was a toddler. He deserves to move on from this world for everything that he's done.

Adrenaline rushes through my veins, and I dart forward, my fist raised and my other arm poised to protect me. He snakes to my left side and swings his leg in a graceful arc at my head. I duck sharply and narrowly avoid the sole of his boot colliding with my jaw. A smile spreads across his lips. Of all of the things Laurings can do, his dangerous grin scares me the most. But it also gives me confidence. It is the sign of a man who is being complacent.

He runs at me head-on and throws two punches directed at my upper chest. I block them both with my arms, and pain lances across the elbow of the arm I'd dislocated earlier. I absorb the hits as best I can, gritting my teeth at the contact. I send my knee flying into his chest, and he gasps, lurching backward.

As I'd expected, he quickly recovers and jumps towards me again, using his strength to his advantage. He sends another punch at me, this one directed at my head. I snake to the right, using the footwork that I've perfected in training for years. As I duck his punch, I drive my fist into his lower chin, catching him right below his jaw. It collides with him, and he stumbles back. I rush forward at him, using the two blows I've landed on him as motivation.

Laurings rolls to the side as I send a kick toward him then comes out from behind me and swings his leg at my face. I duck a second too late, and his boot collides hard with my jaw. Blood gushes from my lip, and a deep aching pain erupts in my mouth. The pain causes me to stumble away from Laurings, and I fall hard onto the steel floor of the platform. My vision begins to blur, but I force it back into focus. I know what I'm fighting for. I will not be defeated by this man.

I whip my arms behind me and backflip onto my feet. Laurings comes right at me, and I leap to the side, deftly avoiding a kick to the groin. He lets out an almost animal-like growl and launches his leg at me in a wide sweep. He kicks my legs out from under me, and I fall to the floor. He snakes forward and wraps his arm around my neck in a headlock. I struggle, choking as my airflow is cut off. In a desperate attempt to free myself, I manage to send my elbow hard into his ribcage. The impact forces him to release me, and I turn to jump on him, not waiting for my breath to return fully.

He rolls, but I anticipate the move. As he does, I send the full weight of my body careening into him. Both of us slide to the left, towards the railing. I manage to grab hold of the metal bars, but he does as well. I slam my foot as hard as I can into his hand, but he manages to hold on. The wind threatens to blow us both off. Laurings loses grip of the railing with one hand, but the other is still on it. He tries to regain his grip with his other hand but I kick it back down, forcing him to hang with one hand. He curses, and then I send my foot down at him again, but he narrowly avoids it by sliding several inches to the right.

"The twin files," he rasps, his weak voice sounding nothing like his usual condescending and cocky tone. "Look inside them, and you will find my true purpose."

I ignore his words in the heat of the moment, nothing but the urge to end this fight filling my head. I kick him one more time, and his hand flies off. I suck in a breath as his body plummets down to the ground. He hits the hard concrete, and his body splays outwards, his blood-curdling scream echoing out below.

Laurings is dead.

TWENTY-THREE

I don't move for ten minutes. I lie flat on the platform's cold steel floor, exhausted from pulling myself back over the railing. I take long, deep breaths. Sweat pours down my back and falls down my forehead. I close my eyes from exhaustion.

I force them open, and I realize that I need to see Laurings' body again. I need to know that he's dead after all of this.

I push myself shakily to my feet and stumble toward the edge of the platform. Keeping my hands on the metal railing to steady myself, my eyes travel down the length of the satellite structure and land on Laurings' body. It's still there.

His legs are twisted at violent angles that make me shudder. His arms are splayed in a similar way, stretched out on the concrete in the motion of him trying to stop the fall in vain. His mouth is wide open, his face contorted in a scream. His eyes are the most impassive part of it all. Even though it's hard to tell from here, the normal piercing stature of those blue eyes is gone, replaced with nothing but a cold, lifeless gaze.

It's strange to see Laurings like this when his dangerous personality and antics aren't going straight to your head. He looks like he's at rest, peaceful, almost.

This feels wrong. All of this. I'd thought that killing Laurings would provide me with some solace, some satisfaction, even. But all I feel is emptiness, chewing at me like a chasm split straight through my chest. It's not the same pit I'd felt earlier. I'd been scared to face Laurings before, and this sensation is different. I killed him, but nothing has changed.

Then I remember his last words. The twin files, he'd said. Look inside them, and you will find my true purpose.

I don't know what to do. But I need to open them. I take the files from my pocket, staring at the fragile cases of each chip. I steady myself on a console when I reach the data transfer compartment. I pull open the glass panel and carefully insert each file into the cartridge. When they're tightly plugged in, I close the panel.

I work my way back around the platform. I study the screen in front of me. I can do the data extraction.

I sigh with relief. Skye did what she promised to do. I can only hope she's still safe.

I find a small lever located on the panel, imprinted with the text BEGIN DATA EXTRACTION. I stare at it for a moment, realizing this is what I've dedicated the past month of my life to. Skye, Tristan, Oswald, Denis, Thaxter, and countless others have laid down their lives for what I'm about to read.

I pull the lever.

As I do, the data displayed on the large screen is replaced by a wide process bar that indicates how far the system has gotten with extracting the data. It reads two percent on it. Another line of text shows that this is going to take seven more minutes.

I wait. I swear it takes an entire lifetime.

The screen flashes once more as the file finishes processing the data. The world around me seems to stop.

TWIN FILES
NORTH AMERICAN INTELLIGENCE SERVICE
DATA FILES 337 AND 338

The following information is highly classified. Unauthorized spread of the disclosed information is punishable by death.

Entry #1:

Tuesday, March 17th, 2029

Re: Project Skyfall

From: NAIS Vice Director Evelyn Taylor, Commissioner of Operation Bright Dawn

To: NAIS High Command

Two months ago, Dr. Hazel Sebrand of the Earth Studies Department discovered a tremor causing turbulence in San Francisco, California. We checked all accounts of potential sources for earthquakes near California, and we found none. I ordered a further investigation into this, and we discovered a crater forming in the ocean, nearly three hundred miles off of the Californian coast. After extensive research, our scientists have discovered that this crater was created as a result of an unrecorded skirmish between an American naval fleet and a group of Korean fighter jets during the early 2000s. There is evidence that the two sides engaged in a battle that involved the use of nuclear warheads.

We are the first to discover this, as it has gone unnoticed for several decades. Our chief geographical team analyzed the situation, and we have come to the conclusion that ninety-one percent of the earth will become uninhabitable within the next decade. We have run advanced computer analytics, and the board has mutually agreed to begin working on Project Skyfall.

Some may label us as traitors to humanity, but we consider ourselves the most likely to survive this global apocalypse. Construction has already begun on a highly classified city built high in the Appalachian mountains. This plot of land is predicted to be one of the last standing landmarks on the planet, and we call it Skyfall.

We have dedicated many resources to it and have come up with a blueprint that will allow two million people to live there at once. We have selected this small population using an algorithm, and these chosen people will be transported to the city by the winter of 2038. The rest of the world's population will, unfortunately, be left to fend for themselves, as we do not have the resources to form cities like this for the global population. Some may consider this brutal, but we consider it the survival of the fittest. We may choose to keep this information from agents for their own safety and for the confidentiality of Operation Bright Dawn and its overseers. Humanity's survival rests in our hands, and sacrifices need to be made in order for some of us to survive.

- Taylor

Entry #2:

Friday, September 28th, 2034

Re: Project Skyfall

From: NAIS Vice Director Evelyn Taylor, Commissioner of Operation Bright Dawn

To: NAIS High Command

R&D reported an issue with the project. A former NAIS agent named Oscar Laurings has somehow gotten word of this project. He's recognized by our inner circles as the killer of Nicolas Reed. His organization calls themselves the Shadow Group, and as far as we can tell, they are a growing legion of mercenaries and talented fighters. They've begun sabotaging supply runs to Skyfall and have severely slowed down our progress. We've contacted Interpol and several other national intelligence agencies and have labeled Laurings as an international criminal. All agents are ordered to fire on this man should they find him. Some NAIS agents believe that his morals are greater than ours; we must eliminate him before he can become a larger problem.

For the good of humanity.

- Taylor

TWENTY-FOUR

A tear in the earth's crust is slowly destroying the land from the inside out.

A city in the Appalachians meant for people deemed necessary for the survival of the human race.

The disregard for the billions of innocent people not on that list.

It takes me a moment to comprehend the details.

Each line of text flashes like a storm in my mind.

And Laurings.

He was fighting for something right.

I put my head in my hands. I want to hit something; I don't have the energy to. This is different. I hadn't expected this. Part of me questions how the NAIS has so much power and how it could be so corrupt. I've belonged to the organization since I was fifteen years old, six years total now. Has my entire life been a lie? Has there always been something sinister lying underneath the NAIS' stainless veneer?

I walk back to the railing.

A tear slides down my cheek.

I killed a good man today.

I look at his dead body. I close my eyes. The anger wells up.

I just take a deep breath.

I will make it right.

EPILOGUE

ONE MONTH LATER
THE ALPS

I place one finger on the metal plate that now covers part of my face. My eyes stray upwards to the mirror that lies hooked onto the smooth gray wall. I can't get used to this—the curved metal sheet that is wedged into the place where my left cheek used to be. I can feel several wires running along the plate as well and onto my jaw.

I then glance downward at the mirror, and where my right leg used to be lies a long artificial metal leg, the joint covered with machinery and wires. The leg is supposed to be synced to my brain so that it should work like my left leg does. A brace is tied around my hip and wraps down onto the leg, meant to keep it more stable. I try to flex it, and it works well enough. Burn marks cover my arms in random spots. I grimace.

I turn away from the mirror, tired of my new reflection. I'm in a large room with three gray walls, one large floor-to-ceiling glass window, and barely any furniture at all other than two armchairs and this mirror.

"A crater seems to have formed in the earth's crust," says an unfamiliar voice.

I turn to find that the glass window at the end of the room is displaying the news. It's like an advanced invisible TV, using special hologram technology.

"Yesterday, a massive tsunami hit the coast of San Francisco. The president has been evacuated, but close to ten thousand people were killed."

The screen flickers off, transforming back into a window. A man stands outside, his arms folded. He walks around and opens the door. As he steps in, he lets a cold breeze blow into the room.

"Hunter. You've been in here for a week," Chanson says, shaking his head.

"There are different things that you could be doing, you know. I know you're upset about your father, and I'm sorry about that." He pauses.

I look away from him. On the day I had woken from my coma, I had first asked about him.

I remember the deep pain I felt when Chanson said, "I'm sorry, Hunter."

I had openly cried, something I do very rarely. Father had worked all for the greater good, no matter what those NAIS fools had to say about it.

The room opens out onto a balcony, and I head out onto it, Chanson at my side.

A cool breeze is now blowing across the mountaintop, ruffling my hair. Snow-capped mountains lie in front of me in either direction. I try to smile. When I do, I can feel the plate moving to work with my cheekbone and jaw. It tingles, and it soon turns into a small, gnawing pain. I release the half-hearted grin.

I turn left and head down a set of stairs. My metal leg easily bends at the knee, adjusting to the steps just like my other leg does. The ground opens onto a grassy slope dotted with snow at random intervals. A metal fence lies at the edge.

I want to try something. I was told my new leg would make my movement quicker and stronger.

At first, I ease into a slow jog. The leg creaks and whines slightly at first then stops as I pick up my pace. Now I speed up to a sprint. The metal leg almost seems to carry me. I'm faster.

I stop running. I'm not even panting. I look down at the metal leg. Maybe it's not too bad after all.

I stare down at the glacier in front of me. It reminds me severely of his death. I don't look away. He died with honor, defending the people he loved and what he thought was right.

My mind cannot accept his death. I think for a long time, leaning my elbows gently onto the glass railing, staring at the icy field below me.

August Gilman.

The single person that is responsible for my father's death.

He cannot be forgiven.

He cannot be let go.

He killed my father, and he will pay for it.

Everyone he loves will suffer, and as he watches his world burn, he will die with it.

Now I know what I must do. I say it aloud.

"I will avenge you, father."

TO BE CONTINUED.

AUTHOR BIO

Lucas Kawamoto loves reading and writing, swimming, and watching basketball. Lucas is inspired to write large-scale stories reflecting the essence of human nature through action and dystopian narratives. He is in ninth grade and lives in California with his parents and younger brother. He plans to continue writing dystopian novels throughout high school.